FALLEN IDOLS

FALLEN IDOLS

June Arrington Wood

iUniverse, Inc.
New York   Bloomington

Fallen Idols

iUniverse books may be ordered through booksellers or by contacting:

*iUniverse
1663 Liberty Drive
Bloomington, IN 47403
www.iuniverse.com
1-800-Authors (1-800-288-4677)*

*Because of the dynamic nature of the Internet, any Web addresses or links
contained in this book may have changed since publication and may no longer be
valid. The views expressed in this work are solely those of the author and do not
necessarily reflect the views of the publisher, and the publisher hereby disclaims
any responsibility for them.*

*ISBN: 978-1-4401-4371-7 (pbk)
ISBN: 978-1-4401-4372-4 (ebk)*

Printed in the United States of America

iUniverse rev. date: 6/8/2009

Chapter 1 – Rescued Again

"Get me out of this place or get them out."

"Charlotte, be quiet. It's all right - we're all here," Mom said, as she straightened my covers. "I can't bear looking at that leg in a cast, hanging in the air like that, but I am thankful you're alive."

Such love was unbelievable. How could they keep coming back for more? I opened my eyes and saw, again, the familiar setting of the hospital room. Did these rooms never change? How many times have I been here? I was having a hard time remembering or maybe I did not want to remember. I looked at the faces looking back at me. They showed the marks from years of hurting. Could

I dare gather the strength to give them hope, again? I was so tired, tired of the secrets.

Stephen, my brother, knelt close to me. He looked as if his heart was breaking. "Charlotte, you know we love you. We don't know what you've been through, but this is not the answer." His words brought tears to my eyes.

I looked at my slender, handsome, brother and whispered through my tears --"It's so hard-- I just can't get it right." I knew he only wanted the best for me. If wishing or praying for something could make it happen, then; I would be whole.

Stephen's wife, Debbie, was not quite as understanding. I could tell what she was thinking just by looking at the deep color in her pale complexion. Her bright red hair was pulled into a bun that drew her face up tight. I had heard Debbie encourage Stephen to give up on me long ago and go on with his life. I knew Debbie had not been reared in a Christian home with love or compassion. Her dad left when she was very young. I knew Stephen did not believe in giving up on anyone and had certainly proven that with me and with Debbie. I believe Debbie had tried to be supportive, but I could tell by looking at her, this was way too much.

Truthfully, I know Debbie feels guilty for feeling like she does. I believe, deep down, Debbie would probably be relieved if I had succeeded in this suicide attempt. After all, I have heard Debbie say on different occasions, "What does Charlotte have to be so upset about? She's been reared in a loving, Christian home in a secure atmosphere with family support." I realized I had never really had it together since Debbie had met me.

"Stephen" Debbie said, "I believe it would be better for all of you, if I excused myself. This is a family matter, and I can't be much help. You guys have got to do something."

I could see Debbie was not making any attempt to hide her frustration over the problem and she was angry with Stephen for sticking up for me. It breaks my heart to think of how much opportunity I have had and how I have floundered it all. I remember our happy childhood and what a great life we had – at least, until I was fifteen. I had definitely changed then. It was a miracle I finished college and got my degree in education.

Here I am, twenty-eight years old and no answers to satisfy the longing in my heart. I knew Stephen didn't have all the details of this new episode yet, but I knew he could pretty much surmise what had happened.

I was amazed at Stephen's kindness when he said, "Yes, you go Honey; I'll be along in an hour or so."

"All right, Stephen, just don't stay forever. She's in good hands; as you know, she's been here before," Debbie exclaimed as she left the room hurriedly.

"The poor thing" Mom said. "She never had the chance to experience a real family -- all the good and bad."

"Mom, she's doing the best she can. I love her and I know she loves me. You only see one side of her and she puts up a barrier to protect herself from the world. I know the real Debbie, and she is a great person with a lot of love locked up."

"Well son, if anyone can get that love out, I know God can help you do it."

I noticed he leaned in closer to Mom. "Right now, I think we need to talk about what we're going to do for Charlotte, Mom. I am almost out of ideas."

"I know Stephen, I am too. I'm, also, concerned about your dad. You know Charlotte is so special to him and these last years have been hard on him seeing her so unhappy," Mom said as she wiped the tear that ran down her cheek.

"Oh Mom, is he worse?" Stephen asked. "What can I do? I'm sorry I have been so consumed with Charlotte's problems and trying to help Debbie learn to trust, I guess I have gotten out of touch concerning Dad."

"Just try to spend a little more time with him, Stephen. With the mini strokes, his speech was affected; now, his mind is so bad he can hardly remember my name," Mom said, as she was now sobbing.

"Mom, I feel rotten that I have not been more helpful to you. Looking at him, I can see the changes and how much worse he has gotten. I know it's more for me that you want us to spend time together. You're afraid I'll live with regret after . . . the thought of not being able to tell Dad . . . I love him breaks my heart. You know I think he is the best man in the whole world."

Stephen walked over placing his hand on Dad's shoulder. "Hey Dad, how're you feeling?" Stephen said as he watched Dad's head moving - back and forth - back and forth - from me to the monitor.

"Doesn't she look beautiful, Stephen?"

"Yes, Dad, she looks great. The doctor says she's going to be all right."

"I don't like it when she looks so sad. Why is she crying, Stephen?" Dad said slowly and distinctly. It seemed to take great effort to get the words from his brain to his mouth.

"Don't worry about Charlotte, Dad. You know how strong she is. She knows how much we love her and that God loves her," Stephen said with some doubt.

"Stephen, can you help me, please" Dad asked with some intensity.

"Sure Dad, what do you need?"

"I think I need to go to the restroom, but I can't remember where it is," Dad whispered as Stephen looked down and I realized with him, it was too late. I could see him grieving for Dad, almost gone.

"Here, let me help you," Stephen said as he brushed his own tears away.

Mom took care of me and Stephen took Dad to the restroom. I knew this was almost more than Stephen could bear. I thought of how Mom had wanted to tell Stephen how bad Dad had gotten, but every time they visited, Dad always seemed to be taking a nap and she couldn't get the words to come out. Mom was probably in denial herself up until today. I could tell, now, that Mom realized it was time to do something. Something had to be done. Where do they go from here? What is the right thing to do at a time like this? It was too much to think about.

"Right now, young lady, we have to concentrate on you. What is it you need, dear Charlotte, to make you smile? It saddens me that you never let Jesus into your life. I realize now, it was partly our fault. When we moved to Chatsworth, you were only thirteen. We didn't take the time we needed to find the right church. Remember when our neighbors, Mr. & Mrs. Johnson invited us to church. We went without finding out what kind of church it was. We saw they had an active youth department and the church made us feel welcome and we did not realize it was more a social gathering than a church. When you turned fifteen, you lost interest completely in the church and we found a good gospel preaching church, but it seemed it was too late for you."

"It wasn't your fault, Mom. It was something else. Do you remember I was always trying something new? I remember your face when you found out I had dabbled in marijuana and you talked to me about the dangers of getting into drugs. I remember saying to you, 'Mom, when I'm grown and I have kids, I am never going to ride them like you do me and Stephen. I'm going to let my child make his own decisions.'"

"I remember trying to explain to you that children left alone; without parental guidance usually make the wrong choices. You seemed determined to prove me wrong. You tried to prove that those with guidance can go astray. You constantly broke your curfew or would slip out when everyone was asleep to meet your friends."

As I watched Mom's grief stricken face, I was so ashamed. Then; there was Dad. I saw what happened earlier, even though Stephen had tried to hide it from me. My dear, precious Dad, so sick, and me in no condition to help him. I keep thinking of all the great times we had together when I was a child. Not one of my friends had a family like mine. They would always ask if they could come over and spend the night at our house.

"Mom, I remember how you always had a home-cooked meal in the evening. We would sit around the table for an hour talking with each other about our day. I remember Dad always having a story for us. It was so much fun. He always told a story with a happy ending, and then gave us a moral lesson to be learned from the story."

"Where did those days go? What changed at our house?" Mom asked.

"When I heard Stephen praying for me today, I realized you guys have been praying for me from the day I was born. I know, now, how much you all love me. Well Mom, looks like He answered your prayers again -- and for what -- another let down -- another disappointment?"

"Charlotte, I know you are weak now from surgery, but soon, we are going to talk about what happened to you thirteen years ago. It's been way too long and you have to finally face it and move on with your life. I don't want to seem harsh, but you need closure."

Oh yeah, I knew what had happened to make me bitter and hardhearted. I could see his face now in my mind's eye. I could never forgive him for what he put me through. The heartache, guilt and scars were too deep to ever heal. I knew I needed more time to think it through before I told anyone about it. Mom left to get dinner and I decided to take a trip down memory lane and finally try to come to grips with everything that had happened. I knew I needed to tell someone but I knew it could not be Dad.

Chapter 2 – The Pain of Remembering

I remember being a typical, carefree, thirteen-year old thinking he is a hunk, as they said back then. I probably flirted with him, like all the girls did. He didn't seem to mind - we were just young girls having a good time at church. He had a beautiful wife and a darling three-year-old daughter. I remember how all the girls tried to embarrass him and make his face turn red. He seemed so innocent and naïve, and loved joking with us. We were young and full of ourselves - what did we know? Mom and Dad always taught us to trust. I had never encountered anyone that would want to hurt me.

Little did I know that my youth pastor, Chad Everett, had a secret place at his house that he kept locked at all times. In that secret place were pictures of all the girls in our youth department. Not school pictures -- no -- pictures he took when we were not watching -- catching us at youth functions. He was a master at it! He would set us all up for a game or a race in the pool and tell us he was going to take some pictures for the bulletin board in our department. He usually had a few shots displayed, but he always got a few great pictures for his private collection, I found out the hard way.

"Boy, did I find out the hard way." I realized I had spoken aloud to no one. I believe now that Chad knew what he was doing from the very beginning. He probably started out thinking he would never act on his fantasies. It was just a secret he enjoyed all alone. I remember how he told us why he became a youth director. He said he didn't get much direction when he went away to college and his family was more than glad to see him leave home. The idea came to him, he said, when everyone kept asking what he was majoring in. He didn't know, so he would say he liked young people and they would exclaim, "Oh, I see, you're training to be a youth pastor!"

"I see now why it was a good fit for him." This was getting scary, talking out loud to myself. I digress. Chad had a career that paid his salary and was able to be around all the young girls he wanted. Of course, he needed a wife to be a youth director to add balance to his life and take away any suspicion that might fall on him. He was a respectable married man with a darling, baby girl. The perfect set up. What a fool I was!

It seems now to me that Chad made sure I was always around. I remember how Chad would say, "Charlotte, you are the best baby-sitter we have found. We want you on a regular basis." I heard him tell his wife, Paula, how great I was with Emily and how I was always so agreeable and polite. He said I would be a good influence on her. He bragged about me constantly to my folks - told them all the things parents like to hear. They trusted him implicitly, as I did.

I loved Chad and Paula and especially, Emily. I remember when they would stay out late; I would sleep in the guest room. I'd put Emily down, watch a little TV and go to bed. When they came in to check on me, it was all very innocent. Chad, sometimes, reached over to tuck the covers close to me and get me laughing by tickling me. It didn't seem odd to me because Paula would come in and we'd all sit and talk about some upcoming event. They treated me like family and I remember how my brother tickled me all the time. I trusted him completely. What I did not know was the thrill that Chad felt every time he touched me. I remember thinking Chad treats me just like Stephen does; always with kindness and respect. He joked with me and pulled tricks on me. I really belonged and was loved, or so I thought. I found out later how he would sneak back into the room and take pictures of me. I was the main character on display in the secret place.

I remember when Paula got pregnant again. I didn't know until much later that Chad was not happy about that. Yes, he said all the right things to her to make her feel loved and beautiful. I guess he thought he had to keep up the image.

When it was time for the baby to arrive, they asked me to stay in their home to care for Emily. It was summertime, I didn't have a job and my family agreed. Emily was five and no trouble to care for. The birth took nearly twenty-four hours so Chad stayed and when little Ethan finally arrived, he came home and crashed. He slept all day and when he awoke, he went to see Emily, and of course, me.

When he came outside, the two of us were in the pool he had installed the month before. After greeting us and hugging Emily; he told us all about Ethan and showed us his birth picture. He was very handsome.

It was hot and Chad said he was going to change clothes and come join us in the pool. In a few minutes he came out of the house with snacks and colas. We got out and sat around the picnic table in the shade. We teased Emily about dunking her in the pool. Emily knew we wouldn't since we both loved her. She was not the least bit worried. Emily walked over to the pool, turned and motioned for us to come in with her. I remember I felt a little hesitant about it, but Chad said I was part of the family and I had to go in since Emily was the boss. We all laughed and jumped in to cool off.

Chad wanted to play a game where we lifted Emily into the air and throw her as far as we could. Since she could swim and was not afraid she delighted in the idea. We each took an arm and a leg and swung her back and forth, back and forth and released her. After releasing Emily, I remember slipping in the water and was falling. Chad grabbed me.

After regaining my balance and composure, I noticed that Chad was still holding on. Not like my brother and

Dad, but in a different way. It didn't necessarily feel bad - it was kind of nice. This handsome man that I loved, as a brother, was standing behind me with his arms around my waist. I told him I was all right and he could let go.

Chad said very quietly, "Suppose I don't want to let go?" At first, I thought he was in one of his silly moods and was going to throw me down in the water -- just picking on me to make Emily laugh.

"Chad, you had better not throw me in this water. My hair will get wet and I will have to wash it before church tonight." Chad was not laughing now. He held me close and moved his hands over me. I had never been touched like this before by him or anyone else. I pulled away and went to Emily, who had been playing at the shallow end. I told her it was time for her nap and that we had to go inside.

After Emily was bathed and changed and I had dressed, we went up to Emily's room. Chad was in the room when we got there and I remember stepping back for a moment.

Chad asked me to please come in and said a silent "I'm sorry" and told me he would like to read Emily a story before she went to sleep. While Chad read her story - I went to the guest room and packed my clothes.

When he came down and saw I intended to go home, he asked me to sit down. He needed to talk to me, he said. Chad proceeded to tell me that he could think of nothing but me. Whether he was awake or asleep, I was on his mind and in his dreams. He was crazy about me but he had an idea that might work for both of us.

"I think I should go home, Chad, I don't like this kind of talk - not from you - not from someone I've known forever and I love like a brother. Please don't say those things - take them back - go back to where we were" I begged.

"It's too late to go back - I can't - I need to kiss you; just once - please Charlotte. Just kiss me and I'll get Emily up and we'll take you home," Chad promised.

I did care for him. I guess I always had, but until now, I believed it was all an innocent flirtation - one that all young girls have on their leaders - their teachers - their coaches. What could be the harm in a single kiss? After all, I had hugged and kissed Chad and Paula on many occasions; of course, never on the mouth, but could that be so different? I remember I was so afraid of losing him as a friend. "You promise things can go back the way they were with just one quick kiss," I said. I knew it did not seem right, but this was a man I trusted with every part of my life. He is not a bad man - he is a good man. If we could get pass this moment - I wouldn't have to lose him, Paula and the children, I remember thinking. It will be just like it's always been. Chad promised me again that it would be just one kiss and he would take me home.

"All right," I whispered as I walked toward him. He asked me to put my hands on his shoulders. I had never been kissed but I had seen it on TV and had seen Mom and Dad kiss all my life. Their kisses always seemed innocent enough. Perhaps this would not be a bad experience after all. I smiled at him and said, "Let's do this."

I noticed Chad was not smiling. He had a strange look in his eyes -- his breathing had changed. I pulled back and dropped my hands to my side. "This is not a good idea," I whimpered.

"It's a very good idea" Chad said to me as he grabbed me and pulled me close to him and kissed me passionately. Only he did not stop with one kiss. He continued holding me and touching me where he shouldn't. He threw me to the floor and I remember crying and trying to pull away, but he was no longer the gentle, kind, friend I had known. He was a beast -- a hungry beast -- who could not be satisfied.

When it was over, I was in a state of shock. He dressed himself and told me to take a shower. After I was dressed, he came into the room and said, "You realize, you can never tell anyone this happened."

"I will so tell. I'll tell Mom and I'll tell Pastor what kind of monster you are."

"No one will believe you" Chad smirked, "and even if they believe you -- they will think it was your fault. Everyone knows how you practically live here these days. How many girls have you talked to about me? Don't you see I'm a man of the church, with a family? I've been through so much these last few weeks. I come home and you're practically naked in the pool -- you invite me in -- we play with Emily -- she'll tell everyone -- I mean you are a gorgeous girl. Every man will look at you and say in his mind he wished it had been him instead of me. They won't say it out loud but that's what they will think -- and the wives -- oh, what they will say about you has never been said."

All of a sudden -- I knew he was telling the truth. How did it look? How had it looked for a long time? How stupid I had been – why had my parents let me be here this much?

He fixed us a cold drink, while I sat speechless. What happens now, I wondered? What had he done to my life? Was it ruined forever? He pulled out pictures of me in my swimsuit, others of me sleeping in the guest room. I was so stunned he finally reached over and slapped my face to bring me back to the present. He told me to get my stuff together. "You don't have to worry about me ever touching you again. You are now damaged goods." I couldn't believe this was the man I had admired all these years. Emily awoke and came in laughing and talking about the great time she had in the pool with us. Chad looked at me slyly and winked.

They took me home and as I walked toward my room, Mom asked if I felt well. Chad said he thought I might be coming down with a bug; and with his wife and new baby coming home tomorrow, he decided it was best if I came home. Mom let me stay in bed a few days, feeding me chicken soup and babying me. I needed that.

I remember trying to pick up my life. It was no use; life had no meaning. I was sullen all the time. I smiled only when I had to convince Dad or Mom I was okay. I started going out with friends and staying busy. I didn't want to be available to baby-sit in case Paula asked me. She did ask a few times, but each time I got out of it.

I knew Paula could not understand what had happened to sweet Charlotte. That smiling, happy, face was nowhere to be seen. I found out later that Chad told her it was just a phase all teenagers go through. They get moody and obstinate. Didn't she remember being like that when she was young?

I remember thinking my life was over when I found out a few months later, I was carrying Chad's child. What do I do now? Where do I turn? I couldn't bring that shame on my parents. They had tried so hard to raise me right. I remember going to my guidance counselor at school and telling her my problem. She suggested I get an abortion and no one would ever have to know, not even my parents. I guess I considered it for a moment, but knew I couldn't kill another human being. When Mrs. Carlson realized I would not get an abortion, she set me up with a group that handles adoptions. I remember thinking about how I was going to hide this from my family. I pretended not to care about my weight and went on a food eating binge. Mom was worried about me but Dad said he was glad to see me eating again. I had been so depressed for months; he thought it was a good sign.

As the time progressed, I bought loose fitting clothes and was not around my family much. I made every excuse to be out of the house most of the time. I basically slept there and would leave early in the morning, not returning until late. The adoption agency made sure I saw a doctor and took vitamins. They found a family that wanted a child and they paid all my expenses.

When I was about eight months along, I had my guidance counselor contact my parents and tell them there was a program that lasted for one month that would help me when I graduated. I could go to this facility and help take care of the elderly and that would get me some credits I needed to graduate. After much pleading and begging from me, they agreed. I actually went to live with the family that was adopting my baby.

I grieve every time I think of it. The labor was so hard – I was so frightened and alone. I never thought of God or about what I was doing to myself. If only I had turned to my family, I know, now, they would have been there for me. I was too ashamed and I did not want Chad to know about the baby.

I went home after that ordeal and tried to go on with my life. By the time I was in the eleventh grade, I had experimented with several different drugs and alcohol. I loved the way it made me feel: nothing. I could forget for a few hours. The guilt I carried about how it was partly my fault about the rape, and the grief for a child I had given away ate at me every day. The hate I felt for Chad was all I could feel as it grew day by day.

I went to church when I had no other choice. My family was concerned for me and had recently changed churches as they were not happy with the church they were attending. Since they had never reared a daughter and had heard such horror stories about teenagers growing up, they assumed it was something that would pass with time and I would grow out of it.

I filled my days and nights with school activities in my senior year. I served on every committee that would have me. I became the life of the party -- and the prom queen. My parents had never let me go to prom; but what they did not know would not hurt them.

Graduation was over and I was out of there. Maybe going away to college would help me forget; help me heal. That did not happen. I joined the party group and was only sober on school days, and once in awhile, not even on those days. I held it together long enough to get my teaching degree. I wanted to be a great teacher like my brother. I was hired to teach fifth grade in a town near my home. I could never go back there to live. I worked really hard at settling in and doing a good job. My party friends from college were gone. What could I do now? Working every day - grading papers - and doing lesson plans was not cutting it for me. I had to have something else. I needed to forget.

There was no way I would have a relationship with a man. I was ruined for life from that first and only experience. I was estranged from my family, my choice. I had no church and I didn't want one. I was so lonely, even in a crowd of people. My heart ached for something, but I didn't know what. I hadn't known a normal life since I was fifteen. In my mind, on that day, I lost more than my innocence. I lost my soul and spirit. There was nothing left for me. That was when I tried to end it all the first time.

When I didn't show for school one morning and had not called in, one of the teachers began to worry about me. She had noticed how restless and anxious I was. She told me later she assumed it was first-year jitters. She asked her teacher's helper to watch her class and drove the five miles to my apartment. When she couldn't get me to the door and saw my car parked outside, she asked the super to open the door. There I was -- lying in bed -- pale -- clammy to the touch. She felt for a pulse; found one and my life was saved because of that teacher's concern.

Not that I appreciated it. I was sent to a center for drug addicts and to group counseling. I lost my teaching job and was never able to get enough control of my life to get another one.

I worked at one fast food place and then another, making just enough money to buy the drugs and booze I had to have. There was no getting around it now, I had to have them. It got to the point I would do anything to score.

They were not relationships - they were my next fix. It was easier than working at McDonald's and didn't take near as long to earn enough. I had no guilt over it. I was long past feeling anything. It was a business proposition - that's all it was.

The next time I tried it-- I thought I should use a gun but I knew nothing about them. I asked one of my 'business partners' if he could get me one. "For the right payment, I can get you anything you want." he said. That had been very difficult for me, but he did give me the gun.

I took it home and held it near my heart (or so I thought) and pulled the trigger. I didn't know the little twenty-two couldn't do much damage. It knocked me down and I went blank for a moment, thinking I had finally succeeded -- soon I would be free.

I lay there on the floor and my mind wandered of thoughts of Mom and Dad. I remembered, as a child, how much I was loved and thought of all the stories Dad told us. I came to myself realizing I did not want to die and reached for the phone.

The ambulance came and took me to the hospital. Since this was another attempt at suicide, I was, once again, placed in a secure facility for my own safety. I stayed there a few months. I got drug-free and actually smiled, occasionally. My parents were very attentive and took me home with them hoping this would help. Stephen had married and he and Debbie came whenever they could. They still went to church twice on Sunday and Wednesday nights and they invited me to go, but I told them I couldn't face anyone yet. "I need more time," I begged.

Because of the drugs and not eating regularly, I had lost a lot of weight. I was very pale, and my rib bones showed through my clothes. Gradually, I put on a few pounds and had a healthy glow. I felt, almost, at peace. Maybe I could make it after all. I knew it would make my parents happy and would thrill Stephen. I knew Dad was not doing well but I was so distraught over my life I found it hard to think of anyone else's.

I finally gathered enough courage to drive into town and I would go on different occasions to the library and sit for hours with a good book. It seemed my life was finally coming together. But, I remember now, today was different. Today, I saw him. He was sitting at a table with several young girls. He had to be close to forty. He had tried to keep that boyish look by combing his hair over to hide his bald spot. I remember getting sick, and before I knew what was happening -- I was throwing up everywhere. Everyone took notice -- of course -- and the smell was disgusting. I wanted to die right there.

Then Chad saw me. I saw him excuse himself and walk toward me. They said, "ooohhh" and "aaahh" as he left the table to join me.

"Well, well, if it isn't Charlotte. I wondered what happened to you. Now I see," he said with a sneer.

"Leave me alone," I said as I looked for a table to crawl under.

"You bet I'll leave you alone. You see that bunch of cuties over there - they all think I'm the greatest."

I started to say something, but he held up his hand and said. "You remember that feeling, don't you Charlotte?" He spat out my name. "I will give you credit for one thing, though. You were prettier than any of them" He looked at me in disgust and said, "Look at you now. Have you seen yourself in a mirror lately? You look forty years old - you can't be thirty yet. What in the world happened to you?"

"You happened to me -- you hypocrite -- you deceiver -- you are Satan himself," I yelled.

He grabbed my hand to quieten me and sat down. "You don't mean that few minutes, how many years ago now, did this to you?" He looked as if he felt a moment of guilt, but it quickly passed. His conscience had been seared many years ago. "You don't think you are going to mess up what I have going, do you? I have to admit it doesn't have quite the thrill it used to have. Maybe I need to change my MO - add a little something else. I have to be careful though, make sure they don't have any marks. Hey, you wouldn't believe how many little innocent looking girls are not so innocent anymore. I can't afford to take something home to Paula. She's been acting very peculiar lately anyway."

I remember I sat looking at him -- speechless -- just like that day, long ago, in his house.

"Get out of here now so they can clean up your filthy mess, and just to set the record straight, you were my first. If you had just cooperated that could have been a pleasant experience for both of us -- but no -- you had to freak out on me. Remember, I got what I wanted. You were nothing to me ever. My wife really liked you. Of course, she likes all my girls. I only pick the best of the crop, and you were it for that moment in time" he chided. "Get out of my sight - you make me sick to look at you and you smell worse."

I remember getting to my feet and stumbling from the library and finding my car. I don't remember turning the ignition, but soon I was flying down the highway. I saw the long bridge up ahead and I must have sped up. When I got to the middle, I guess I turned the wheel sharply and hit the bridge rail head on. The car flipped over the bridge and landed in the water. There were two fishermen on the riverbank when the car went over. They saw me and jumped in to save me. They pulled me to safety. I had a big gash on my head from the windshield; I had some internal injuries from the air bag and a broken leg.

And here I am again. Why am I still here? Do I really have a purpose? Can I ever have peace? Maybe there is a God after all. There was always a guardian angel there to save me. Where did they come from?

Chapter 3 – Coming to Grips

"Sweetie, are you all right?" Mom asked tenderly.

"Yes Mom, I'm finally awake. I've been asleep for over thirteen years. I'm awake now and I know what I have to do."

"What do you mean you've been asleep, honey?"

"It's a long story, Mom, and when I'm a little stronger, I will tell you and Stephen. I don't want Dad to know - he doesn't need to hear this" I realized I was shedding tears, real tears, real pain, reliving all of it; but I needed to relive it so I could begin to heal and move on with my life.

The Police looked at it as an accident, not drug related and a few days later, I'm in my old room where I grew up. It's painful to remember my sleepless nights there, but now that I am awake, I have to face it all. My leg's in a cast, but it's coming off in a few weeks.

Mom, Stephen, Debbie and I talked for hours. I shared that day thirteen years ago with them and all the things that followed. At first they were full of questions -- almost blaming me because I had not come to them and told them when it happened. "Maybe we could have done something about it," Stephen said. I tried to explain it the way Chad had explained it to me and finally, they understood why I would have been afraid to tell.

Chad's in jail now in the Atlanta Federal Penitentiary. The detectives are gathering evidence against him. It seemed when I was brave enough to talk, it loosened the tongues of quite a few more women and young girls.

Chapter 4 – I believe I will make it

A few months later, Chad was in court and faced his accusers. He was convicted on twenty-six counts of minor sexual abuse.

It was hard to see Paula in the courthouse. She looked so sad for the girls he had abused and seemed to realize what she had always known, down in her heart, something was wrong, but didn't want to admit it.

I started staying with Dad at the assisted living facility. He had continued to deteriorate, and that was the only option we had. Mom sold the house and we rented an apartment near the center. I wanted to see Dad every day and make sure he received the care he deserved. I started back to church and was going with Mom to a group therapy class. It wasn't long before I was able to ask Jesus to come in and make me His child.

Stephen and Debbie had a little boy and named him after Dad, Thomas Stephen III. Debbie seemed so happy and content now. She looked at me with new eyes. When she heard what I had been through and could, finally, do the right thing, she said she knew she could find forgiveness in her heart for her dad and truly learn to trust again.

I look toward my future now with excitement. I am getting the training I need to go to the assisted living center and care for all the elderly that need me. I know now that Mom's and Stephen's prayers have been answered. I, now, have a purpose, I have peace, and I have passion. I am so glad to be awake!

Chapter 5 - CHAD SPEAKS:

Chad could not believe it had finally happened. His pride had gotten him caught. He could not resist gloating to Charlotte. It had just been too tempting not to belittle her in front of his girls. He, of course, would not have done it if he had known she was going to freak out. He could not imagine how that few minutes with him over thirteen years ago, could have affected her life so dramatically. It was enough to make him stop and think of the many others. How had their lives been affected? Were they all in this dire distress he saw written on Charlotte's face? For just a moment, he regretted many of the things he had done.

The real truth was that for more than twenty years, he had not given much thought to anyone, except for being able to get what he wanted from them.

Paula was a wonderful woman and it was hard to sit in that courtroom day after day and see her tears, to see her shock and shame because of all the things he had done. No, that had not been a pleasant experience. He was glad when it was over. It amazed him to see all these girls he had molested in some way. Now that he had been found guilty, he didn't expect to ever have to face them again. That much was a relief.

With all his sins, he really did love his children. He was glad Paula had not let Emily, eighteen now, or Ethan, only thirteen, come to the courthouse. He knew she would never let them see him again. He couldn't blame her. He hoped what had happened would not affect them the rest of their lives -- as it had him.

Chad let his mind wander back to the time that he had hoped never to revisit. When he left home at fifteen, he swore he would never look back. His dad had died when he was only two. He had been brought to his mother's bed to bring her comfort from that day until he turned fifteen. He realized when he was about ten that something was wrong with his Mom. She acted like he was her husband, instead of her son. Having no one as a role model, Chad thought it must be normal. After so many years, he could not stay any longer. He never told anyone about it. He was too ashamed. If only someone had been able to help him, maybe........

Thinking more clearly now, he realized that no one could have helped him. They did not know the circumstance. He had gone to live with his dad's brother, Uncle Joe. They knew he was troubled but they chalked it up to being raised without a father and with no exposure to the church or religion. Uncle Joe had taken him to church and had put up with all the havoc he caused in his family until he graduated high school. With Uncle Joe's help, they had been able to get him into college with some religious courses. Chad assumed it was like a last ditch effort at helping him put his life together. That is where he met Paula.

Chad remembered how kind and loving Paula was to everyone she met. He was very attracted to her, and after he had made the decision to be a youth pastor, he believed she would be a great asset to him. Chad realized for the first time that even in making that decision, he had been thinking of himself.

Suddenly, all the sins he had committed weighed heavily on him. He felt as if his heart was going to burst. Maybe this is what people feel when they have a heart attack. One thing for sure, he would have plenty of time to think about all the disgusting things he had done. He could not get the faces of his victims out of his dreams. Seeing them helpless and frightened had been so exhilarating before, but now he only awoke trembling with shame. He had been sentenced to twenty-five years in prison. There might be a chance of parole after fifteen if he could prove he was rehabilitated. He had only served six months. Will the nightmares never stop? Would he have to see those faces night after night, would he ever find peace?

The last time he had seen Paula was in the courtroom on the day he was sentenced. He wondered how she and the children were doing. He hoped their friends at church had not blamed them for his sins. He hoped they were still accepted and could go on with their life. He wished every day he had taken his own life years ago and saved them all this shame and hurt.

Prison life was very hard to endure. The Atlanta Federal Penitentiary was known for the hard criminals there. It was a high-security prison for men that opened in 1902. It was the site of an 11-day riot when Cuban refugees from the Mariel Boatlift were tired of being detained. Past inmates included mob boss, John Gotti and Carlo Ponzi, mastermind behind the infamous "Ponzi Scheme." It housed over 2,000 inmates with 600 staffers.

The things that happened to him were indescribable. He did not want to think of those things. Many of the prisoners heard about his crimes and they had their own way of making him pay. Chad believed he deserved the punishment he was receiving, both from the court and from these prisoners. He gave up and was a walking shadow of a man. He had nothing to live for, but was afraid to die. He knew his sins were many and he tried to think back to the many sermons he had heard from the pastor. He couldn't even remember what he had taught the teenagers. Was he so far in sin that he only said what he thought was right to them? He usually had his eye on a new target and his thoughts had been consumed with them.

What a waste -- what a travesty. So many lives he could have touched for good, but instead, he had been a roadblock to them ever finding the truth.

The truth -- what a concept -- what is the truth? His mind was so damaged with sin; he didn't think he would recognize truth if he heard it.

Chapter 6 – Help is on the way

"Jill, do you know where my New Testament is?" Chris asked his wife of fifteen years. Chris and Jill were members of a local church in the Atlanta area.

"I think I saw it in the bathroom. Perhaps it was your reading material this morning," Jill teased as she rubbed her hand over his recently shaven head.

"Yeah, yeah, tease me if you will. I get a lot of good reading done in there," Chris said as he reached for her hand.

"Have I told you today how blessed I am? Having you as my wife and three wonderful children -- God is so good."

"Yes, I think you told me at lunch, but I never tire hearing it. Right now, you'd better get ready to go and meet Nathan. You know he's always early to church. He seems to be enjoying this soul winning training more than you, if that's possible."

"Jill, I believe you're trying to get rid of me. Yes, Nathan is really picking up the 13-point plan quickly. We're only into session three and he is getting anxious for me to be the 'silent' partner while we are winning people to Christ. It truly is exciting -- watching new converts learn how to bring someone to Christ when they have only been saved a few months themselves."

"Isn't that what Dr. Wood says in the very first session?" Jill asked as Chris was getting into his jacket. Jill knew that Chris was very acquainted with Dr. Wood.

"Yes, first, we are to present the Gospel and help bring a soul to Christ. Then, we are to help disciple them and get them baptized. Then, we are to teach and train our new convert to go and do for someone else, what was done for them. It is a wonderful concept and gets the new convert into soul winning immediately."

"Well, the children and I will be praying for you this afternoon as you go to the prison witnessing. We will pray that someone will be hungry to hear about redemption and forgiveness. I hope you get the opportunity to present the Gospel in a clear and concise manner and that Satan will be bound and not able to interrupt your message," Jill said with great conviction.

"Thanks Sweetie, I'll tell you all about it when I get home," Chris said as he kissed her gently on the forehead and left the house.

Chapter 7 – The Prison Experience

"Hey, Brother Nathan, did you have a good day at work?" Chris asked his soul winning partner. Nathan had just started working with a big computer company.

"You bet. I really like my new job. I have to admit, though, I couldn't stop thinking about our opportunity tonight. Didn't you tell me that you have been trying to get into that prison and have a ministry among the prisoners for months?"

"Yes, our church has been working with the prison officials trying to clear the way. It finally happened last week, and we are allowed to go twice a week for an hour. Isn't that wonderful? Jill and the children assured me they would be praying for God's blessings tonight as we go," Chris said, as they got into his car.

"Then we can only have good results if your wife is praying for us. I have always admired the relationship she seems to have with the Lord. I know if I had a problem, I believe she would be one of the people I would want praying for me in time of trouble," Nathan commented as he fastened his seat belt.

"Speaking of praying -- why don't we do that right now? Will you lead us to the Lord, Nathan?"

"Dear Lord, we have so much praise you for. Thank you for your love, your mercy, and your forgiveness. Thank you for Chris and thank you for sending him into my home and for telling me about you, Lord. Especially for tonight, we ask for your guidance, your protection, and for your power as we talk to these prisoners. Lord, I know there are hurting men there -- unsaved men who need you -- lead us to them -- open their hearts -- even now -- and prepare them for your Word. In Jesus name, I pray, Amen."

Chris and Nathan continued on into the Atlanta traffic to the prison. Chris felt a heaviness of heart and prayed that God would direct him to the one that needed God and that he would say what God wanted him to say.

Chapter 8 - Redemption's Plan

"OK, you lazy bums. You can leave your cells for an hour if you want to get preached to by that church that will not leave us alone. It's your choice -- we don't care one way or the other. They will be coming twice a week. Don't get any funny ideas about trying to escape. The guards will be with you all the time. If you behave yourself this time, maybe we'll let you go again on Sunday," the guard growled at them as he rattled their cell doors with his Billy stick.

Most of the prisoners liked to get out of the cell anytime they could. Someone could be conducting a quilting party, and they would go. Chad was both excited and angry that someone had come to preach to them.

He was sure they would rant and rave about what rotten sinners they were. He could hear it now, but like the man said, what did he have better to do?

As they marched into the meeting room, they heard a song playing on the little CD player the two men had brought. The melody was familiar to Chad -- what was the name of that song? Something about the cross and me being on His mind -- yes, that's it. 'When He was on the Cross, I was on His Mind.' It seemed a holy hush came upon the room as they found their seats.

After the song, one of the guys, the young one, got up and talked about a recent experience he had that changed his life forever. You had to give it to him, Chad thought, he was sincere. He talked about God's love that had taken a filthy sinner like him and shown him what He had done on Calvary for him. Jesus had paid all the debt he owed for his sin. In all of Chad's life, he had never heard a testimony like that.

Chad decided that, at least, he could listen to the other guy as he got up to speak. He introduced himself as Chris and told of a similar salvation experience. He told them how he had deserved death and Hell because of his sin. Chris told them, "I'd like to read Romans 3:23, that says all of us have sinned, and that we fall short of pleasing God no matter how good we are."

Chad wanted to ask him some questions but did not lift his hand. Maybe they will have questions later, he thought.

"Now, the Bible say in Romans 6:23 that the wages of sin is death and that we individually do not deserve Heaven, but Hell." Chris noticed how attentive the men were being and was surprised. He then shared, "Now in Romans 5:8, it says that God commended or proved His love toward us, in that while we were yet sinners, Christ died for us." He explained how much God loved mankind, how that in God's sight there was no little sinner or big sinner. "I want to assure you that no matter what you have done – no matter how bad or seemingly unforgivable; God loved you so much, He sent His Son, Jesus, to die in your place – to pay your sin debt."

Then Chris read Romans 10:13 – "For whosoever shall call upon the name of the Lord shall be saved." There was no maybe about it. It was for sure. "If you are willing to admit that you are a sinner and want to accept the death of Jesus as payment for your sin and if you will pray and ask Jesus to come into your heart and save you, then you will be saved and on your way to Heaven."

Can this be true? Can this really happen to a man like me? I've done things this man could never even imagine. It can't be me he's talking to, can it? Chad wondered.

"Let's bow our heads in prayer and let me lead us," Chris said.

By this time, you could have heard the softest cry. That little room had become a holy sanctuary, full of the presence of God.

Chris asked God to bless these men and to help them see their need for a living Savior. He prayed they would be willing to trust Him with their lives, and that they would open their hearts and receive His forgiveness.

Chad was trembling; he didn't know if he could continue to stand. He held onto the chair in front of him. He felt the convicting power of God in that room and in his heart.

When Chris asked the men to raise their hands if they would like to know this Jesus he was talking about, several of the men lifted their hands. Chris and Nathan were rejoicing in their hearts. They knew God was doing a mighty work in someone's life right then.

Chad lifted his hand along with the others. Chris then told them he was going to say a sinner's prayer for them to pray, so they could let Jesus into their life and find forgiveness. He asked them to repeat the words that he prayed, but assured them they were not praying to him or Nathan, but to a living Savior, who had died on the cross 2,000 years ago. He assured them if they had been the only person on this earth that God had loved them so much He still would have sent His son, Jesus, to earth, and then to the cross.

Chad had never heard of this kind of love. He had a hard time believing it was that simple. There had to be more to it than this.

At first, his prayer was one of desperation. He had nowhere else to turn; he could not continue living like he was now. He had to have help. He would give Jesus a try and trust Him with his life. He certainly did not have anything to offer in return to Jesus, for His forgiveness.

Chris told them they just needed to repent of their sin and ask for forgiveness, and then accept the free gift of salvation, and they would be saved with the promise of Heaven when they died.

Chad prayed that prayer Thursday afternoon. Chris and Nathan rejoiced with those that accepted Christ and promised they would be back Sunday afternoon and bring more literature that would help them begin to grow in their spiritual life.

Chad walked back to his cell a changed man. He had never felt peace and joy in his entire life. There was nothing he had ever done that made him feel what he felt right now. It was beyond words. He knew he wanted to know a lot more about this man, Jesus. It was strange how he had worked in a church for years, and had never seen anything like he had witnessed tonight in that little meeting room. He decided then and there that he wanted to meet with this man, Chris, in a private meeting. He wanted to tell him what he had been convicted of and share with him that he was having trouble believing God would save someone like him. He knew he was forgiven -- but he wanted to know more. He needed to know more.

Chapter 9 - A Few Weeks Later

"This has turned into a bigger commitment than you had imagined, hasn't it, Chris?" Jill was happy to hear of the great results her husband and Nathan had at the prison a few weeks earlier, but it seemed now, Chris was at the prison all the time.

"Yes, sweetheart, can you believe what God is doing there? We had several that received Christ, but this one guy, Chad, really got a good dose of God's love. The last few weeks he has been so full of questions, we hardly had time to teach or help the other converts. He is so hungry to learn and just soaks up everything he hears. Isn't that great?"

"Yes, it is wonderful, and I'm happy for him, but you know you haven't been here very much lately. What happened to twice a week at the prison?" Jill did not want to seem selfish, but she missed him when he was gone.

"Well, Jill, Chad has become such a changed man that the prison officials called the church and said we could come out whenever we wanted. I guess it's making their job easier with a group of Christians in their cells witnessing and sharing Christ with the other inmates."

"Does that mean you and Nathan are the only ones that can go from our church? Don't we have others that can share the load?" By this time, Jill was feeling guilty over not being 100% as positive as Chris was to ministering to these new converts.

"Sweetie, you know we are finishing up our thirteen-week session of Operation Go next week. That will put more men out in the field. It is our first time at the church to go through this program. Because Dr. Wood created this program for the local church years ago, and the fact that I grew up around it all my life makes it a reasonable assumption that the pastor wants me to continue with Nathan at the prison right now. It won't always be this way. Chad has such a hunger that I have taken the personal responsibility to teach him the thirteen-point plan, step-by-step, so he can be an effective witness for Christ. He has many more years to serve in the penitentiary and I know God is going to use him in a mighty way.

We are in our second week of training at the prison this week. In the plan, the trainer is supposed to go on visitation three hours each week with his new convert so he can learn how to tell others about the Savior. The guards are letting us meet with the different prisoners and some of the guards are accepting Christ. I am so honored to be a part of something this exciting. To see a life wrecked by sin and then to see a man that is now on fire for God; a man that now has a reason to live, a reason to wake up in the morning is a miracle that only God could have performed. I only have about ten weeks left until Chad will be totally trained and then he will be able to be on his own at the prison. Can you even imagine what God can do through one man that is totally surrendered to God's will for his life?"

"Oh, Chris, I'm sorry. I was being selfish. I am happy for Chad and his new life in Christ. You go and do what you need to do for him. The children I will keep you more earnestly in our prayers. I know in a few weeks there will be others at the church ready to help out in this great endeavor the church is undertaking. Perhaps I should pray about going to the next 13-week session that's offered in the fall."

"Jill, it is the one thing that has changed my life the most since I became a Christian. You would love how it takes away the fear of witnessing. It gives you boldness you never thought you had. I do think you should pray about going through the next session. I can't wait to see how Nathan is going to do as a trainer. He was a great trainee and actually was instrumental in seeing five folks come to know Christ in the thirteen weeks. That doesn't count the dozen or more we've had saved at the prison. Oh, by the way, did I tell you, Nathan met someone?"

"You don't mean it? Are we talking about the same shy, Nathan, who can't talk to women? Who is it? How did he meet her?"

"Whoa Jill, don't start planning the wedding. Remember a couple weeks ago, when Nathan went to that singles retreat down in Savannah? Well, he met this woman that he said was so easy to talk to and found out she lives about sixty miles from here. Her name is Charlotte and Nathan says she works at some assisted living facility for the elderly. He seems to really like her as her name comes up quite often."

"Has he seen her again since the retreat?" Jill asked all excited. Nathan was one of her favorite people. He was a little over thirty and she thought he would make a very good husband to some woman. She would definitely be in prayer about that situation -- but she wouldn't buy a wedding present yet.

"Yes, I think he went over last week on his day off and took her to lunch. He doesn't know a lot about her yet, but he is interested in knowing more."

Chapter 10 - Charlotte Finding Her Way

Charlotte could not believe it had only been a little over a year since she had reported Chad to the police. So much had happened; she now had a nephew that she loved dearly. Stephen and Debbie lived in Savannah with his new teaching job. She was so glad to see Debbie as a new mom. She had never seen her as happy and content.

The fact that Charlotte had finally settled her eternity with Christ and found joy in her new life made all the difference in her outlook on life in general. She loved her job and had been promoted to manager. She would now interview applicants for jobs and assist with their training. There always seemed to be such a turn-over in this kind of work. She could see it was hard on the residents to have staff in and out so much. She had some ideas about some job incentives that she was going to present to the owners of the center. Perhaps she could do something to keep more of the staff. Charlotte could tell from watching her dad how he would get used to a certain staff person and would start looking forward to their shift and spending time with them. If that person left the job for one reason or another, it affected her dad for days. He would ask about them several times per day. It broke Charlotte's heart to see this happen to other residents also.

Charlotte was glad she and her mom had found a new church close to their apartment. Her mom had gotten involved and was teaching a Bible study course for women and was singing in the choir. Charlotte's job kept her from attending some services, but she had fallen in love with the singles department.

Charlotte had made several friends at her new church. One of them, Rachel, asked her if she would like to go to a singles retreat in Savannah. They could split the cost of a hotel and the gas. It was Charlotte's weekend off from work and she thought she would love to go. "Rachel, I have an idea. We could stay at my brother's home in Savannah and I can visit my new nephew, Thomas. How does that sound?"

"In that case, I will buy all the gas for the trip. Call your brother -- we are headed to Savannah next weekend."

What a great weekend it had been, Charlotte reminisced. Seeing her brother and her new nephew brought to her remembrance how much fun a family can have. The retreat was wonderful with great music and good preaching. She had enjoyed all the skits, food and activities. She had especially enjoyed meeting Nathan in the long food line; a shy man, and so soft-spoken. He was different in so many ways from most men. They had talked in generalities -- about the retreat and about where they were from. She was delighted when she realized they lived only sixty miles apart. Nathan had seemed happy about that, also.

Charlotte was surprised last weekend when Nathan called and asked if he could come and take her to lunch. With everything that had happened to her and then just this year trying to put her life back together, she didn't know if she should pursue a relationship just yet. She really couldn't see how having lunch with someone could be considered a real date. Perhaps she owed it to herself and to Nathan to see if there was any chance for at least a great friendship between two Christians, both committed to living for God.

She had said yes to his offer for lunch. He took her to one of her favorite little restaurants and they spent a couple of hours just talking and laughing. It felt good to have someone to talk to who did not know her past. It would be a long time before she could share that part of her life with Nathan, if ever. It was still too vivid in her mind and she knew with God's help, she was growing in her faith daily – perhaps, someday she would tell him. Her cell phone rang, and she was deep in thought. "Hello"

"Hi Charlotte -- this is Nathan. Did I catch you at a bad time?"

"Oh, hi Nathan -- no -- it's not a bad time. I'm driving home from work. Thanks again for lunch last week."

"It was my pleasure. That's the reason I'm calling. I want to see you again."

"Wow, where is that shy man I met in Savannah?"

"Hey, I'm taking a course at my church to give me boldness in witnessing. I'm trying it out on you. How'd I do?"

"Good enough to make me say, yes. I would love to see you again. What did you have in mind?"

"Do you have next weekend off?"

"Yes, I do."

"Great, we are having a guest speaker at our church. He actually is the man that created the soul winning program I am taking at my church and there is a final banquet and get together. They want us to bring a guest, and of course, I thought of you. Interested?"

"I'd like that, but wouldn't I get home awfully late Saturday night?"

"This brings me to my next question. How about you driving over Friday afternoon and stay till Sunday?

There's a hotel close by and I can register you. Saturday, we can see some sites in Atlanta and go to the banquet Saturday night and you can go to church with me Sunday morning. Can you work that out?"

"It sounds very good. It will be nice to get away a couple of days. I haven't been to Atlanta in a long time."

Chapter 11 - Charlotte's surprise

And finally, it's Friday, and I am really going, Charlotte thought. After talking with her mom, she felt it was the right thing to do. The look on mom's face was priceless when she told her she was thinking of going to Atlanta for the weekend and spend some time with her new friend, Nathan.

"Oh Charlotte, another one of my prayers have been answered."

"Now what have you been praying for, Mom?"

"That you would meet a wonderful, Christian man that could bring some joy to your life; you have come so far in this last year, but I know God has great plans for you. Give this man a chance and by the way, when do I get to meet him?"

Mom and Dad had always been such a blessing to her. Dad was going downhill physically and mentally. She was glad mom was there to spend some extra time with him while she was gone.

Charlotte arrived about 6 PM and checked in. She had dinner in the hotel and was able to spend a leisurely evening catching up on her reading. Nathan told her he was going on visitation with his trainer. It was their last night of the Operation Go program that he was taking. They graduated on Saturday night and he did not feel he should miss the opportunity to go out with Chris again.

Charlotte met Nathan in the restaurant at 9 AM for breakfast. Then, it was off to see several interesting places. "I love underground Atlanta; all the restaurants and interesting vendors," Charlotte said. "I never realized there was so much to see at Stone Mountain, either. I'm glad we came."

The day flew by and now it was time for the banquet. Nathan picked her up and told her he was anxious for her to meet his soul winning partner, Chris, and his wife, Jill. She could tell he really admired the man. The food was great, and she really liked Nathan's friends. They sat together and Charlotte got the impression from Jill, she was really happy that Nathan had a date.

The music was inspirational. She felt the presence of the Lord in this assembly of believers. Before the message from Dr. Wood, the pastor asked several of the teams to give some memorable events in the past thirteen weeks from their visits. Several stood and gave their statistics. Then, Chris stood and gave several statistics that were very impressive. He and Nathan had won forty-nine folks to the Lord and ten of them had come to church and gotten baptized. Chris spoke with such fervor, "Pastor, I know there's no way that everyone here can tell everything about our visits, but with your permission, I have a specific situation that includes praise and a prayer request."

The Pastor nodded and Chris continued. "It all began, when we were able to go to the prison here in town about ten weeks ago. Our first visit there was so amazing. I still have a hard time comprehending what happened. We presented the salvation plan to about fifteen men. They listened respectfully, and then we extended an invitation for them to accept Christ. Several hands were raised, but my eyes settled on a man that we could see was visibly trembling, so much so, that we thought he might be having a seizure. He finally knelt, but we could tell he had questions on his mind. Then we watched as the power of the Holy Spirit worked in his heart, and we saw him totally surrender himself to God. I have to tell you I haven't seen that kind of conviction or surrender many times in my life. After receiving Christ, that first visit, he became so anxious to hear more and was so changed that the warden called the church and asked us to come back whenever we could. My praise is that this man was gloriously saved and now for ten weeks I have been going back at least twice per week to ground him in the Word and teach him this thirteen-point plan."

Suddenly, the room was full of clapping and rejoicing. "My prayer request is for this man. He has such a love for God now and wants to be used by God to reach other inmates for Christ. He has served less than a year of a twenty-five year sentence. He wants us to pray for him that God would use him mightily as he starts several Bible studies. He says God has forgiven the worst of sinners when He forgave him and he wants to make up for some of the hurt and shame he inflicted on his victims. He gave me permission to use his name so you can pray for him. His name is Chad Everett. I know only a little about his past, but undoubtedly, he hurt quite a few people before he was caught."

"Charlotte, are you all right? Charlotte, can I get you something? You are as white as a ghost. Do you have a health problem I need to know about?"

Nathan was offering her something to drink -- calling for a cold washcloth for her face but Charlotte could only stare into space and could not answer him.

Nathan and Jill helped her to his car. Charlotte was shaking all over and Nathan gave her his coat. "Do you want to go to the hospital, Charlotte?"

Charlotte moved her head back and forth to say no. Nathan drove her to the hotel and helped her to her room. He was not leaving her alone. He helped her under the covers to get warm and sat down in the chair beside the bed. Charlotte lay still and could not seem to close her eyes. Nathan was beginning to worry and asked her did she want him to call her mom. She moved her head from side to side again to say no.

Nathan had his New Testament with him. He took it out and started reading one Psalm after the other aloud to Charlotte. Gradually, Charlotte stopped shaking and was able to focus on Nathan sitting in the chair next to her bed. She had no idea how long she had been here. She glanced at the clock on the nightstand and saw it was almost midnight.

"I'm sorry -- it's so late," she said. "You should go -- you have early church -- I'm all right now. Sorry, I ruined your evening."

"Charlotte, you did not ruin my evening. I am worried about you. Do you know what brought on that episode? Can I get you something, or call someone? I'm not leaving you like this if I have to sit in this chair all night long," Nathan told her emphatically.

How could she tell him? It was too soon in their relationship. She had not been able to even tell her family until a year ago. Nathan was almost a stranger. What would he think?

"Nathan, there is something I'm going to have to tell you, but I can't tonight. I'm not up to it yet. Please don't worry about me. I will sleep in tomorrow and then I'm driving home. When I'm ready and if you still want to see me again, I'd like to share my story with you. Can you live with that explanation for now?"

"Of course I can. We won't talk about it anymore; but just to be sure you are all right, I'm staying until you are sleep. Okay?"

Charlotte got out of bed and went to the restroom. She came out a few minutes later in a comfortable sweat suit and laid her head back on the pillow. She looked at Nathan and could not believe the kind of man he had turned out to be; not judgmental -- not nosey -- not scared of her -- even in her fragile state.

"Why don't I read a bit more while you relax enough to go to sleep?" Nathan asked.

"I'd like that Nathan. Thank you for not asking questions. You must think your new friend is a real basket case."

"My new-found friend is just that -- a friend, and the Bible says a friend loves at all times. Now you close those beautiful eyes and go to sleep. I'll leave when you're asleep, but I'm calling you tomorrow night to make sure you got home safely."

"Thanks for everything Nathan," Charlotte whispered as she was finally coming down from her adrenaline rush.

Nathan read a few more Psalms to her and soon she was asleep. Nathan watched as she slept and wondered who could've hurt this beautiful woman so badly that she was scarred permanently. He offered a prayer to God for her and quietly left the room.

Chapter 12 - The Reckoning

Driving home to Chatsworth was almost impossible. Charlotte missed her exit and had to go another five miles to get home on the back roads.

'Why Lord, why is this happening? I'm still new at this. I've only been saved a year myself. I can't bear this yet.'

"My peace I give unto you, my child"

'Lord -- I don't feel any peace -- I'm so confused.'

"I give you my peace when you fully learn to trust me"

'Lord, I really have been trying. You know I have. I thought I was doing so well. What is it you want from me?"

"Love your enemy -- forgive those that have sinned against you."

'What are you saying, Lord? No way, Lord! He ruined my life -- he took away my childhood -- my innocence -- fifteen years of my life. You expect me to forgive him for that just because he got religion? I cannot do that -- I'll never forgive him.'

The whisper of God's Spirit moved away. Charlotte was not ready yet. She needed to be reminded of God's love and what He gave. She needed more convincing. Her time would come -- He was patient with His children.

For the rest of Sunday and Monday, Charlotte walked in a fog -- she was on auto pilot. She spoke only when spoken to and ate only a few bites of food. Was she losing her mind, along with everything else she had lost? She remembered Nathan had called Sunday night. She could not remember what they talked about.

It was Friday already and Charlotte knew she had interviews today for new staff. Their background checks had already been done. She needed two new staff but she had five applicants. She wanted a clear mind and prayed for guidance in making her decision. It was odd how she had hardly thought of God this week. She didn't remember reading her Bible, and she did miss that sweet fellowship with the Lord each day. Charlotte remembered how precious her time with God each day had become.

Would she ever have that relationship with Him again, she wondered?

When Charlotte arrived at 9 AM, the business manager handed her the applications and told her one of the applicants was waiting outside her door. Charlotte greeted the applicant -- unlocked the door and laid the applications on her desk. She was chatting with the pretty little blonde girl about the weather and about her level of education. "I've just finished high school, and I want to be a nurse. My mom does not have the money for me to go to college so I'm going to work a couple of years and try to save enough to go," the young lady said.

By this time, Charlotte had made coffee and poured a cup for her and the young lady. "I know who you are and I'm afraid you won't hire me when you know who I am," she said apprehensively.

Charlotte thought she looked vaguely familiar and thought perhaps she had seen her at church in passing. She picked up the applications, and thumbed through them.

'Oh God – no - what are you trying to do to me?'

"Emily Everett, that's my name. I promise I did not know you worked here. When I saw you walk through that door, I was afraid you would recognize me and not even give me a chance at getting this job. I don't blame you if you don't hire me. I really want to work here with the elderly while I save money for school," Emily said and then closed her mouth and waited.

"Emily, will you excuse me for a moment? I'll be right back. I need some fresh air," Charlotte said, as she rushed from the office.

'Lord, why -- why are you doing this to me?'

The whisper in the wind said softly, ***"Your ways are not my ways - do not be afraid child - I am here."***

'But Lord -- you're asking too much -- first, Chad is thrown in my face, and now Emily, little Emily -- it's too much. I don't think I could bear to see her every day. It would bring it all back every time I looked at her.'

"My grace is sufficient -- What about Emily, Charlotte. What does she need? Was any of this her fault? Can you be a blessing to her? Can you salvage her youth for her?"

'But God, I'm not strong enough. I barely make it day-to-day myself,' Charlotte whispered. Then she remembered the verse," ***I can do all things through Christ who strengthens me."***

'All right Lord, you win. I know you have a purpose for all of this coming about at this time. I'm not saying I won't fail, but I will try.'

"Child, My strength is made perfect in your weakness."

Charlotte had to admit, it felt wonderful having her fellowship renewed with her Lord. She had missed it. She walked back into her office and Emily was pacing the floor. Charlotte could see the hurt and shame in Emily's eyes. Suddenly, she saw the five year old child that she had loved so dearly. She wrapped her arms around Emily and said, "When can you start?"

Emily was crying and smiling at the same time. She said, "But -- you didn't interview me yet."

"Oh, that's all right -- I had orders from upper management to hire you on the spot. Let's look at the schedule and figure out when you can start training."

Charlotte gave her the forms she needed for her physical and TB test. She told her to report the next Friday after completing the paperwork. They hugged again and Emily left the office, tears still streaming down her face.

"Was that so hard my child?" The Spirit whispered to Charlotte.

Chapter 13 - A New Start

It was a new day and Charlotte was lighthearted. She was making breakfast for mom. She was glad to feel hungry again and was chatting with her mom about Emily.

"I can't explain it. At first, I was so scared I thought I was going to die. I went outside and I talked -- no -- I argued with God – until He got my attention. I thought about what Emily has been through in the last few years. The shame and humiliation she has endured. When I finally surrendered my will to God, the rest was easy."

"God is working in your heart and life, Charlotte. I'm so happy to see you smile again," Mom said as she enjoyed the pancakes and eggs.

The phone was ringing and Charlotte excused herself to answer it. "Hello."

"Hi Charlotte -- this is Nathan. How are you this beautiful Saturday morning?"

"As a matter of fact, Nathan, I am wonderful. How are you?"

"I'm fine Charlotte. It's good to hear that lift in your voice. You were somewhat out of it last Sunday when we talked."

"Did I say something awful? I hardly remember the conversation."

"Oh, you don't remember inviting me over tomorrow to go to church with you? You said you wanted me to meet your mom and take you guys out to lunch."

"Nathan, I may have been out of it, but I don't think I was that far out," Charlotte teased.

"Yeah, you're right. This is my great idea. As you know our thirteen-week training ended last Sunday and we have a few weeks before we start our fall session. I'd like very much to drive over in the morning -- meet you guys at church and spend the day with you. Would that be all right, Charlotte?"

"Let me speak to Mom and make sure she's free."

"Mom, Nathan wants to know--"

"Yes, Charlotte, I'm free -- I've been waiting to meet that new friend of yours. But you tell him, he is not taking us out to eat. I'm cooking him a home-cooked meal tomorrow. I don't imagine he gets many of those."

"Nathan, did you hear her? I think she was saying it loud, so you could hear it for yourself."

"Yes, I did hear it. I like this woman all ready. Give me directions to the church and I'll meet you there."

Charlotte was surprised at how excited she was. She helped clean the house and then she and mom went to the grocery store. Ella wanted this to be a very special occasion, not soon to be forgotten, by Nathan or by her beautiful, smiling daughter.

Chapter 14 - A Sunday to Remember

"This is a great meal, Mrs. White. Thank you for having me here today -- even though I did invite myself," Nathan said as he buttered another homemade biscuit.

Charlotte watched with wonder at where this 6' thin man was putting all this food; funny how relaxed they all were. Nathan really liked her church and her friends. It was nice sitting in church with a man. That was something she had not done except for dad, who was not able to go anymore. Somehow she felt like she had known Nathan a long time. What was it now -- only a month ago they had met at the retreat?

"Please call me Ella, Nathan. We are so glad to have you with us and you are welcome anytime. Isn't that right, Charlotte?"

Charlotte was in deep thought -- going over the last week, and especially her encounter with Emily.

"Earth to Charlotte," Nathan chided her.

"Sorry, Nathan; so much as happened to me since last Saturday night. Perhaps later today, I'll share some of it with you."

"I'd like that, Charlotte. You were telling the truth when you told me your mom was a great cook. She's the best. I'm afraid I eat on the go so much that I have embarrassed myself here in your home."

"Don't be silly, Nathan. I'm glad you're here, and I think you can tell by Mom's face that she's enjoying having you here. She used to cook for my brother, Stephen, and he enjoyed it like you."

"You said he is in Savannah. I believe that's where you were staying when we met. Isn't that right?"

"Yes, he and Debbie and little Thomas live there. He teaches in the local high school. He says he has fallen in love with the city and I can see why. It is very beautiful."

"Now, don't you go getting any ideas about moving and leaving me here all alone," her mom teased.

"No chance of that, Mom. I love our apartment, our new church, my job and being near Dad. I'm not going anywhere."

"That's good to hear," Nathan said. "I am just getting to know your beautiful daughter, Ella. I'm very interested to see where this friendship can lead."

"Boy, I am going to take that course you are taking. Jill told me you were very shy, especially around women," Charlotte laughed, -- a little embarrassed and a little excited about his comments.

Later in the day, Charlotte and Nathan found a Starbucks and settled in with a good latte and a cappuccino. It felt right to Charlotte being here. It was a perfect atmosphere with relaxing music. She was deep in thought again about how she could get used to this.

"Earth to Charlotte," Nathan laughed, reminding her of the lunch together.

"You're going to think I am a dizzy blonde, Nathan. It just feels so right being here, like this. If you knew my life to this point, you'd understand," Charlotte said with trepidation.

"Try me," Nathan said looking at her with kind, understanding eyes.

"What?"

"Try me -- see if I can understand,"

Charlotte tensed and was unsure where to go from here. She was the one that had brought up the past, but was it too soon? Could she trust this man with the most fragile thing in her life -- the secret she had kept for thirteen years from everyone? She didn't know -- what would he think? Maybe he would see it, like most men would -- that she had asked for it from the beginning.

"Charlotte, anyone can tell just from being around you and your mom what kind of folks you are. You are kind, loving and passionate at your job. You have a great relationship with your mom, and you seem to have a deep, abiding relationship with the Lord. I know you have doubts about trusting me with your past, but have you thought about the fact that God may have brought me into your life for a reason? Perhaps it is no more than being a friend that you can lean on and trust -- someone you can confide in and start the healing that needs to be completed. I can tell you've come a long way but there must be more that God wants from you and maybe he knows I can be a blessing to you. If that is His only purpose for us meeting -- then I can live with that. Just look at me as your knight in shining armor -- OK?"

Charlotte drank the last of her latte. She couldn't speak yet, so she just looked at this man; that surely must be a man projecting the image of Jesus to everyone he meets. It was beyond her comprehension how he knew just what to say -- just what she needed to hear today. Yes, as she looked at this man sitting across from her, Charlotte had strings of memories flooding her soul.

"I don't know where to start," Charlotte whispered.

"Start with a happy memory and go from there. God will give you clarity and guidance. Take your time -- I have all night," Nathan spoke tenderly.

So, Charlotte emptied her soul -- starting with story-time around the dinner table when she was a little girl. Nathan recognized this was very difficult for Charlotte, but he could also see it was something she had to do. When she couldn't say anymore and stopped, weeping, Nathan reached and held her hand -- to give her strength and help her know she was not alone. It took nearly two hours for her to share what she had been through in the last fifteen years.

"So Nathan, you see, when I was at your church last week, and Chris asked for prayer for Chad Everett, it was almost more than I could take. He's a man that I hate with everything in me. I don't want people praying for him -- not after all he did to me and to so many others."

Nathan reached his long arms around her small frame and held her. That's what she needed right now, but Nathan felt he knew what it was that God wanted from Charlotte. He wanted her to forgive Chad Everett. He was afraid it would be quite some time before that would happen.

Chapter 15 - Charlotte comes clean

Friday came and Charlotte had forgotten that Emily was reporting for work. When she arrived, Charlotte greeted her and assigned her to her caregiver to acquaint her with the responsibilities she would be assuming. The morning passed quickly and Emily reported back to Charlotte for orientation after lunch.

"Emily, I'm sure this is difficult for you, also. I can't promise I will always respond well to you. It really depends on the day. I'm sure you have days that are better than others."

"I understand Charlotte. I will try to do my job and not end up in your face. Thank you for this opportunity. I told my mom that you hired me and she started crying.

She was moved with compassion for all that you have suffered because of my dad. I understand if you don't want me to mention him to you. We have not been to see him in Atlanta yet. Mom says she doesn't know if she will ever be ready."

"As a matter of fact, Emily, I feel I should tell you something I recently found out about your dad," Charlotte said carefully.

"Is he all right?" Emily asked too quickly. With everything that had happened, she still loved her dad. She had grown up loving him and only found out a year ago about his double life.

"Yes, he's all right, Emily. It seems some men went to the prison and held a meeting and at the end of the meeting, the prisoners were asked if they would like to know Jesus as their Savior. Your dad was one of the prisoners that accepted Christ. My friend told me he has been marvelously changed and is conducting Bible studies at the prison. I could care less myself, but I thought you and your mom might like to know."

"Thank you, Charlotte. I know that was not easy for you. I don't blame you for the way you feel and I wouldn't expect you to forgive him." Emily said, wiping the tears from her face.

"You're right about that. I never will -- I can't -- but I only recently accepted Christ into my life, so I thought you might want to know about your dad."

Charlotte continued with the two-hour orientation, going over the employee handbook, the policies and procedures and a disaster plan. They finished up and said goodbye. Charlotte did not realize the stress level she had been under during that process. She hoped it would not always be that way; she needed to give Emily a chance to be a success.

Chapter 16 - Later that day

"Mom, you'll never guess what Charlotte told me today." Before her mom could get a word in, Emily exclaimed, "Dad got saved in prison and is holding Bible studies for other inmates. Can you believe it? Isn't that great, Mom?"

Paula could not believe her daughter. She did not think it was possible. After all that Chad had done to her and to his own children, plus all the other victims, she knew it was a way of life for him. He could rot in that prison as far as she was concerned. She was surprised at the enthusiasm Emily was expressing talking about him. Paula had made it a point to protect them as much as possible by not allowing them in the courtroom and now for nearly a year, she had barely spoken of him. This had to be the best thing for all of them. Or so she thought. "Emily, you seem very excited about this. You don't have any plans to go see him, do you? I know you're eighteen and can make your own decision about that, but I had no idea you would have any desire to see him."

"I don't know, Mom. It's hard not having him around, he was always good to us, wasn't he?"

"Yes, he was a good dad. I'm sure my attitude toward him has not been fair on you and Ethan. I am very concerned about Ethan. He is at a very precarious age and at this point, he could go good or bad. I've been noticing his attitude lately. We really need to get back into church. This move to a new location has helped some, but I wish we could find a good church."

"Mom, Charlotte told me she just accepted Christ recently. Perhaps we could visit her church. I'll ask her tomorrow at work if she minds if we come visit her. How would you feel about going to church where Charlotte and her mom go?"

"Oh, I don't know Emily. I think it might be too hard on her seeing us in church. It would bring back bad memories for her -- but -- I know Ethan needs to be in a good church right now. Okay, ask her if she minds if we visit."

Chapter 17 - Emily's Request

Emily could hardly remember Charlotte's dad. She had only been five when Charlotte stopped babysitting. It was right after she quit that Charlotte's family had left the church. She enjoyed taking care of Mr. White. That's what she called Charlotte's dad. What a special gentleman he was -- so appreciative of anything done for him. She was glad to have the opportunity to care for him. She stood at Charlotte's office door and knocked with apprehension -- knowing what she was asking Charlotte to do for them.

"Come in, Emily -- how are you today? Does my dad need me?" Charlotte was so attuned to her dad's needs, she was constantly checking to see if he was all right.

"No, he's fine. He had a good breakfast and I just gave my first shower all by myself. He was very cooperative. I'm glad I had such a nice person for my first independent shower without a supervisor. I wanted to see you about something else. I told you we moved recently to this area. Mom thought it best to get us out of the church and school. We have not found a new church yet and I asked Mom if she would like to visit your church. She said I needed to ask you first -- that it might not be what you would want -- of course, we would understand. Ethan is having some discipline problems at home and in the new school. Mom feels he needs to be back in church but he doesn't have much interest. Do you think it would be all right if we visited your church tomorrow? I'm not on duty until 3 PM so we could make the morning service."

'Oh, Lord -- what do I say?'

"My peace I give unto you"

"I have to say, Emily, this thought has never crossed my mind. I don't know how it will feel, but I do know that God would want you and your family in a Gospel preaching church. I believe you would like my church. Of course, please, do come and your mom can see my mom again, and it will be good to see Ethan. He was just an infant the last time I saw him. I will give you the church location."

'What are you trying to teach me, Lord? What more do you want from me? I gave her the job -- I did what you asked -- is that not enough?'

Charlotte was full of anguish and regret Saturday night. Her mom noticed her mood and prayed for her, but did not pry. "Mom, you'll never guess who's coming to church tomorrow."

"Oh, is Nathan coming again? I can tell he really likes you. I like him to."

"No, Mom, it's not Nathan -- even though I wish it were him. Emily Everett asked me today if her family could come visit our church. They haven't found a new church home since they moved to this area and her brother seems to be having some problems. It was very difficult to say they could, but the Lord wouldn't let me say anything else."

Chapter 18 - Ethan's Rebellion

"I don't care what you say. I am not going to church tomorrow." Ethan screamed as he stormed out the front door and jumped on his bike. Ethan was Emily's younger brother that had gotten very bitter over the last year because of his dad.

"I guess that didn't go so well, huh?" Emily could see the hurt and near fear in her mom's face with Ethan's declaration.

"Oh Emily, I'm afraid for Ethan. He has gotten so rebellious and bitter about everything. All of this has been too hard on him. Fourteen is such a hard age in the best of circumstances. I can understand his apprehension about going to church. He is probably still so embarrassed about his dad and thinks the whole world knows about it. We are definitely going to have to pray daily for him. Pray that God will send some circumstance or person into his life to help him come to know the Savior. He has a very tender heart. You remember how gentle he was as a baby and how he adapted well to any situation."

"Yes, Mom, I remember. Look what God did for me, though. Who would have thought He would bring Charlotte back into my life after all these years? It has not only been good for me, it has been good for her, also. She has struggled a lot with God these last few weeks. She told me the other day with so much happening so fast, that dying to self daily wasn't working for her anymore. She said she was telling God she was dying moment by moment."

"Emily, I don't ever remember a time when Ethan trusted Christ as his Savior. Suppose he hasn't and goes out and does something and gets himself killed. Oh, Emily, I could not bear it. It would be my fault for his not going to church recently. At a time when he needed God the most, I have been so absorbed with myself that I have practically ignored him. Remember how we used to read Bible stories and pray together when you were growing up? I can't remember the last time I prayed with Ethan or even prayed for him. Well, that is going to change. Perhaps I won't get him to church in the morning, but I will soon. I have to!"

An idea began to form in Emily's mind. She was going to take Ethan to see Dad. Maybe, if he could see what a changed man Dad had become, it would help bring him to Christ. She decided not to say anything to Mom about it but determined that next week she was taking him. It would be so good to see Dad again.

Chapter 19 - The Confrontation

"I should have held out for more than a steak dinner," Ethan grudgingly said to Emily.

"Since I just started my new job, that's all I can afford right now," Emily told him as they took the exit that would take them to dad. She had gotten directions from someone at work but had still taken two wrong exits. The traffic was so much greater than she was used to.

"How can you look so happy about seeing Dad? Can't you see how he hurt Mom? I have no intention of being nice to him. It's just been a long time since I've had a good, thick, juicy steak," Ethan said to her as they arrived and went to the designated parking area.

They arrived a few minutes before visiting hours began. Ethan watched some men playing basketball, others were weightlifting, and some were just standing around smoking. This place didn't look so bad to him. They looked like they were as happy as he ever felt. In a few minutes they were taken inside and searched. They confiscated his knife, cigarettes and lighter. He laughed when he saw the expression on Emily's face when they searched him.

"What – never saw cigarettes or a knife before?" Ethan said as she stood with her mouth open.

"Not on my baby brother. What are you doing with those things? Does Mom know that you're smoking?"

"I'm sure she will after today," Ethan sneered and walked away.

They were led into another waiting area with many people waiting to see loved ones. In a few moments the door opened and a lot of prisoners marched in. They were given a moments instruction and then were dismissed to visit.

Emily had called ahead so her dad would be ready for them.

Chad could see that Ethan and Emily were in the middle of some altercation but made his way over to them.

"Dad," Emily couldn't get anything else out. She had a lot to say, but did not know where to start.

"Emily, you look wonderful. Did your graduation go all right?" Chad was also at a loss for words. He had waited for this day for months and now that he was seated at a table with them, he did not know where to start. The vibes he was receiving from Ethan were not good ones. "So, Ethan, how are you?"

"Couldn't be better, DAD! Let's see – since I saw you last – I have changed schools, neighborhoods, and friends. I now live in a dumpy apartment and, oh yeah, Mom had to go to work to support us. So Dad, how are you?"

Chad felt the greatest amount of guilt he felt since he received Christ and became a Christian. "Ethan, I'm sorry. I know I have hurt so many people in the last fifteen years - you, Emily, your mom. I know it does not change anything for you, but I want to tell you something that has brought a complete change in my life. Can I tell you about it, guys?"

"No, Chad," Ethan said emphatically. "I don't want to hear it." He got to his feet and walked away from the table.

"I'm sorry Dad. He has been going through a really rough time. Mom doesn't believe that Ethan ever accepted Christ, and now he has no interest in anything to do with the church or family. I'm sorry he called you, Chad. I guess it was his way of getting the message across."

"Yes, I got that loud and clear. I deserve it though. He has no reason to ever forgive me for what I did to him."

"I'd like to hear what happened to you and then I have something to tell you," Emily said with a smile.

Chad began his story with Chris and Nathan coming to the prison.

Emily had never seen her dad so animated. He could hardly sit still as he told of his conversion and the training he received from Chris. He shared what he was doing every day at the prison and told her of the many that were being converted. Chad had his New Testament with him and shared life-changing verses with her. He wept as he spoke of the cross and the price that was paid for his sins. "How He could love me and forgive me, I will never understand, but I know that He has. I only wish it could have happened twenty years ago and my life could have been so different."

"I'm happy for you, Dad, truly I am. God works in mysterious ways in our lives. I told you I had something to tell you – I graduated in June, and I went to a place that takes care of elderly clients. You'll never guess who my boss turned out to be, Charlotte White – can you believe it?"

"She gave you a job? That's a miracle in itself. Tell me how it happened."

Emily shared her times with Charlotte and laughed when she told him that Charlotte hired her without an interview, "Said she had orders from upper management to hire me." She told him that Charlotte had received Christ in the last year. She was off drugs and suicide attempts. She told him about visiting Charlotte's church and how she liked the singles department. Emily also shared with him that Ethan would not attend church with them and that he had with him, today, cigarettes and a pocket knife that the guards had taken.

Chad's heart was heavy. His precious son – his Ethan – so lost. What would it take for him to come to the Savior? He was sure his son would not listen to him. He assured Emily he would pray fervently every day for Ethan.

"I did not tell Mom we were coming here today."

"When you feel the time is right, please tell her you saw me. Tell her I am so sorry and that I'm not anything like the man I used to be. Tell her I will be bathing you all in my prayers, and if she could find it in her heart to forgive me someday, I would love to see her."

"Well, Dad, a lot has happened. I will wait for awhile to tell her. It might be a little hard for her to believe you have changed. I don't mean to hurt you or to doubt you, but it is hard to believe."

"I know, Sweetheart, thank you for coming here today. It's been wonderful seeing both of you. Our time is up for now, so you'd better gather Ethan and leave. Hopefully, I'll see you again soon."

"Bye Dad," Emily said as she took his hands in hers. Tears filled her eyes as she realized how much she missed him. She fell into his embrace and held on to him. The visitor's bell rang, and she turned and left.

Chad watched as she walked to Ethan, and they left the room together. Ethan never once looked his way. His heart was breaking for his son. How lost and alone he must feel. He remembered his own life at fourteen and how desperate he had been. He had no one to talk to so he had kept it all bottled up inside. Chad breathed a prayer to God to please send someone to his son to help him, before he ended up in a place like this.

Ethan was devouring his big, rare, steak with a vengeance. Emily was so angry with him for how he had treated dad. She played with her salad and tried to reason in her mind, how Ethan must feel about his life. She decided not to talk about Dad or their visit. "Is your steak good? I'm afraid you won't be able to digest it. You're swallowing it whole."

"Don't try to pretend you're not angry with me. I saw you hug him. How could you? I'm never having anything to do with him, and I'm never going back to that prison with you."

"We'll see, Ethan, sometimes there are powers at work that are much bigger than we are. I really believe God is going to get your attention, one way or the other. I know I am going to pray for you and I know Mom is everyday. Dad told me he will be praying for each of us every day."

"Look Emily, don't make me say something I will regret later. Knock it off -- I don't want anyone praying for me. I can take care of myself. Most of all, I don't want that hypocrite praying for me."

Chapter 20 - Ethan's Big Brother

Nathan and Charlotte saw each other as often as possible. Since he knew of her past, she shared what Emily had told him about her visit to see her dad. While she spoke of Ethan, Nathan's heart went out to him. How hurt and bitter he must be. He definitely would start praying for Ethan that God would send someone into his life to help him.

Months passed – Ethan was in high school. He met lots of new people and was out of the house most every night. Older guys and girls that had their own cars came and picked him up. He was out of control. He was failing in his subjects and he couldn't wait to be old enough to quit school. The principal asked his mom to come in for a session with him and Ethan.

"Mrs. Everett, I don't know what it is going to take to make Ethan realize he is throwing his life away, day by day. I know a little of your history, and I have given him a break several times, hoping he would appreciate it and come to his senses. It has not helped. He is a whiz on the computer, and he recently inserted a virus which has left our system down. He knows how to fix it but says he won't do it unless we promise to pass him on all his subjects. You know I can't do that. I'm out of ideas except for calling the police and getting them involved. My sensitivity to his situation hasn't helped in the least. Do you have any ideas?"

Paula looked at her long-haired son – dressed like a bum on the street – earrings in both ears – face down and looking at the floor. In her mind's eye, suddenly, she saw her precious two year old on his knees saying his prayers to Jesus. She saw him playing horsy with his sister and remembered that special laugh.

'Lord, what is the answer here? What can I say to help Ethan and also that the principal will agree to? Help me, Lord.'

"Mr. Jackson, didn't I read in your material that you have a Big Brother, Big Sister program here at this school?"

"Yes, we feel it has helped some students. We've had a few successes – real turn-a-rounds – is this the idea you have? You think that could help Ethan?"

"I don't know but we have to try something. Ethan, please wait in the other room while I talk with Mr. Jackson."

"Mr. Jackson, we have a friend who is a computer genius. As a matter of fact, he works for a big computer company. I think if I called him, he would come and fix your computers. I want you to suspend Ethan for one week. I do have a favor to ask. This gentleman that will be fixing your computer could have the greatest influence on Ethan, I believe. Could you let this gentleman be his big brother?"

"That is an unusual request, but if we get some letters of recommendation from his employer, his church, his neighbors, I think we can work this out. I want Ethan to get some help. He's very smart and can be a fine young man if he has some strong direction."

"Thank you, Mr. Jackson. I will do what I can. Thank you for giving him another chance. I will have our friend, Nathan; call in the next couple of days about the computers."

Chapter 21 - Paula's Request

When Paula had met Nathan at church, she was very impressed. She had wanted to ask him to talk with Ethan and see if he could be used of God to help turn Ethan's life around. She had been noticing how much worse he had gotten. She knew he was failing, but he would not study. If she tried to ground him and tell him he had to stay home and do his homework, he laughed in her face and walked out. Perhaps all this happened for a reason. She hoped that Nathan would be willing to help them. She knew it was almost a sixty- mile drive one-way. God would certainly have to be in it to make it come together.

Paula asked off work for a few days for a family emergency. They agreed, and she prayed for God's guidance in dealing with Ethan this week. He had been so frightened of going to jail that he agreed to the Big Brother program. He, of course, did not know who his big brother was going to be. In previous conversation with Nathan, Paula found out he was one of the gentlemen that God had used to reach Chad with the Gospel. Only a few days ago, he told her he was praying for her son. Emily had told Charlotte about the trouble he was getting into all the time and Emily, Charlotte and Nathan placed Ethan on their priority prayer list fearing his future.

Nathan hung up the phone and could not believe what he had just agreed to do. God does work in wondrous ways. He thought about how he had been praying regularly for Ethan for several weeks - praying that God would send someone into his life to help him. Nathan had talked several times with Chad about Ethan. Chad assured him that Ethan would not have anything to do with him, but that he might listen to someone else. He was praying so earnestly and fasting, asking God to send someone. Nathan figured he should not pray for something if he was unwilling to put feet to his prayers if God impressed upon him to do something. Well, it seemed God was asking him to be a blessing to this young man in desperate need.

Chapter 22 - Ethan learns to trust

"Hi, I'm Nathan. I'm going to be your big brother for the rest of the school year."

"Hi. I guess you know my name and have heard what a loser I am at this school. I am not promising anything but I had to do this for my mom so they wouldn't send me to jail. We already have one jail bird in our family. I did not want to add to her misery."

"Well Ethan, I appreciate your concern for your mom. I don't think you are a loser at all. Perhaps you have lost your way for a little while, but I know God can see you through this crisis time in your life. I just want to be a blessing to you."

"And you say you're from my school? I've never met anyone from here that talks like you do. Who are you, really?"

"Let's just say, I am a friend of a friend that cares about you deeply. Listen, Ethan, I have every Wednesday off from work, so we will have to meet then. Is that all right with you?"

"Sure. It doesn't matter to me"

"Great. Well, let's plan on that. I will pick you up after school and we will spend some time playing basketball, skating, or whatever you enjoy doing. We'll talk some and eat a good meal. Then I will be taking you to a local church that has a great youth program on Wednesday nights and I will be one of the workers in that department."

"Hold on a minute now. We didn't say anything about having to go to church. That wasn't part of the deal as far as I am concerned. I'll just ask for a different Big Brother that's not religious."

"I'm sorry, Ethan. That's not going to happen. I'm afraid my orders came from a higher source than your school principal. He had to work very hard to get me assigned to you and I know he will not back down. The truth is we all feel you have great potential but that you just need someone you can open up to and share all the negative feelings and thoughts that you are having right now. You'll see that you'll get used to having me around and hopefully, will start looking forward to Wednesdays."

"What church is it we're going to, anyway?"

"Actually, Ethan, it's the church that your sister and mom have been visiting."

"I should have known it. They have been trying to get me there for weeks and I would not go. Funny how all this worked out, huh?" Ethan said as they said their goodbyes.

Chapter 23 - Charlotte's loss

Emily buzzed and said, "Charlotte, call 911. Your dad is not responding."

Charlotte placed the call and went to her dad's room to wait for the ambulance. She had noticed this morning, when she arrived, he did not seem well. While questioning him, she realized his speech was more impaired and he really didn't seem to know where he was or to recognize her. She had called Hospice right away and they told her they would be there within the hour to check on him. That had been forty-five minutes ago. Charlotte called in extra help and asked Emily to please stay with him. "What happened, Emily?"

"I went to the bathroom and when I returned, I went over to offer him some water but he didn't answer me. I called his name several times but he didn't respond. That's when I buzzed you. Oh Charlotte, is he gone? I've never been around anyone when they died. Is there anything I could have done differently?"

"No, Emily, there was nothing else you could have done. It is his time." Charlotte could see they no longer needed the ambulance. When they arrived, they pronounced him DOA. It looked as if he had a stroke that took his life immediately.

Ella arrived at the center as soon as possible. Thankfully, they had made pre-burial plans so there was not a lot to do. She sat with her husband of over forty years and held his hand. It was still warm to the touch. It was a blessing to see the peace on his face and contentment she had not seen for a long time. She knew he was in the presence of God at that moment and that he did not have to suffer anymore. She knew that even if he could come back to her, he wouldn't after spending time with Jesus in Heaven.

The funeral home sent the hearse to pick up her dad and Charlotte kissed him goodbye for the last time. She, too, could see the peace on his face and she had to smile at him. He was finally home after so many months of insecurity and fear. Alzheimer's was such a cruel disease. It stripped the family of the loved one before he was gone. The patient lost all sense of time and finally in the end, their dignity.

The funeral was on Saturday and Charlotte was touched when she saw Chris and Jill and Nathan come into the funeral home. She was glad she had these new friends. She introduced Chris and Jill to her mom and her brother, Stephen and his wife, Debbie. She told them that Chris was the gentleman that had been instrumental in seeing Chad Everett saved at the prison. They chatted a few minutes and then she saw Emily and Paula arriving with Ethan dragging behind.

Ethan could not believe they had made him come here today. Why did he have to come just because Emily worked for the woman whose dad died? It did not make any sense to him until he looked up and saw Nathan standing with the grieving family.

Then he understood. His mom had chosen this man to be his Big Brother. He had to admit he had a good time on Wednesday with Nathan. He was not pushy at all and he was very athletic. They played basketball and then had a great cheeseburger and fries. Even the youth department had not been so bad. It was different than his old church but he was going to stay distant with them and just act nice for the sake of his mom. She surely had been through enough already.

"Hello, Ethan. I guess you know my secret now, huh?" Nathan said to him. "Perhaps it is better you do know. I felt bad not telling you how all this came about. I'd like to introduce you to some friends of mine. This is Chris and Jill."

"Nice to meet you. You guys live around here?"

"No, Ethan. We live about sixty miles from here. Just a few miles from Nathan," Chris told him.

"Nathan, you live that far away and come to see me every Wednesday? Why would you do that?" Ethan felt disoriented hearing this news.

"We'll talk about it later today. We'd best get into the service now. They are getting the family ready to walk in. We don't want to be late."

Nathan was concerned about Ethan so he asked Paula if could take Ethan out for a coke after the funeral. She agreed, of course.

Paula was glad, in a way, that Ethan now knew how it had come about that Nathan was his Big Brother. She felt she had been deceiving him and wanted him to know it was only because she loved him so much that she had asked Nathan to do that for them. She was happy that she had met Chris and Jill, also. They seemed like a wonderful couple. It was nice seeing Stephen again, after all these years. He had a beautiful wife and son. Perhaps she owed it to the children and maybe to herself to go and see Chad in Atlanta. She would think on it and pray about it.

Chapter 24 - The accident

Chad was in the infirmary getting stitched up from his beating. There were still quite a few prisoners that did not want him telling them his story and then, asking them to accept Jesus into their heart.

"Chad, I know you mean well. We are all very happy about our new found faith and are excited about the many changes we have seen in the lives of many of the prisoners. You are going to have to be careful, though. Not everyone wants to hear the story of your forgiveness. Some don't seem to want forgiveness at all." The nurse was one of the new converts that had been reached. Chad didn't know which one had told her but he was very happy about it.

"Sara, I'm glad you received Christ. It's the greatest thing that has ever happened to me. Have you had a chance to share your faith with anyone else?"

"Chad, my life is so topsy turvey right now, I am barely holding on by a thread. If I did not know I was going to heaven, I don't think I could bear it," Sara said with tears in her eyes.

"I'm sorry Sara. Would it help to talk about it with someone? I'm not much, but I have been through a lot of sin and I know what it can do to a person's life. Getting forgiven and being set free from it is a miracle from God."

"Chad, we're finished patching you up now, so I had better let you go back to your cell. I probably need to talk to someone but I don't know where I would start."

"Would you mind if I ask my friend, Chris or Nathan, to come by one day and see you? They would make an appointment with you and buy you a cup of coffee. I think you would be very comfortable talking with them."

"I think I would like that. As I said, I'm glad I am a Christian but there are some major roadblocks in my life that are defeating me everyday from being what I think a good Christian should be."

"Great, Sara. I will mention it to them. Do you mind if we have a word of prayer for you right now?

"That would be nice, thank you."

Chad prayed for Sara and asked God to be especially near and dear to her in the forth-coming days. He asked for guidance and protection for her. He left her there in the infirmary and that was the last time he saw her.

Sara knew it was only a matter of time until they found her; if only she could go back two years and leave that flash drive where she found it.

Sara remembered feeling uneasy for quite some time at her company in San Francisco. She had walked in on several unannounced meetings and everyone stopped talking. It was only four or five employees involved. So, maybe, they had become friends and were planning an outing together but it just looked suspicious.

That fateful day when she noticed the flash drive on the floor in Mr. Charles's office was the beginning of all the chaos in her life. Why had she been so curious? Look where it had gotten her.

Making a disk from the flash drive had not been the problem. Returning it to Mr. Charles had been the problem. Mr. Charles was in his office, looking around, when she walked in. Why was he there that day? Sara remembered she tried chatting a moment or two, then, she had backed up to the credenza next to the window. She had commented on the lovely view and placed the flash drive under the edge of a stack of folders.

Mr. Charles asked her why she had come to his office. She explained when she noticed he was there that she wanted to remind him of her vacation days coming up next month so he could prepare for her absence. He thanked her and she left the office, sweating profusely.

She knew now why he had looked so worried. He must've found the drive after she left. Sara knew he would be worried about whether she knew what was on it.

Sara didn't have to wait long. When she put the disk in her computer at home, and saw all the information about the overseas bank accounts beside the names of each of the five people that had looked suspicious to her, she knew she was in trouble.

Somehow, they had figured out a way to steal from the company, and it looked as if they had accumulated about $1 million each over the course of about two years. They probably didn't trust each other so they had put all the information on a flash drive as a safety precaution, so none of them could steal more than the other.

'*Why, oh why, did I have to find that? Why did I make a copy? They will kill me if they find out.*' Sara was thinking.

She remembered being so frightened. She caught a plane the next day, traveling 2000 miles from home. Sara found a lawyer in Atlanta and gave him an envelope with the disk in it and told him; if anything ever happened to her, he was to mail the envelope to the address on it.

Next, she e-mailed Mr. Charles and told him she knew what they had done and also, what she had done to ensure her safety. As long as she was safe, the truth would not come out. She found a job in the infirmary at the Federal Penitentiary in Atlanta.

Sara was still always looking over her shoulder. It was hard to feel safe. She had to admit since she talked with Arnie at the prison she had felt more at peace. She couldn't believe something this wonderful was possible in one's life. Why had she never heard the story of Jesus and forgiveness before?

Perhaps she would talk to those friends of Chad's. Maybe they could give her more direction in this new life she had found. Yes, she would look at her schedule and see -- -- -- -- what is that squealing sound -- -- -- -- someone yelling loudly -- -- -- -- she looked just in time to see the big black car crashing into her at full speed.

"She never had a chance," Sergeant Fuller told the EMTs when they arrived on the scene. "One of the witnesses to the accident said he screamed at her to move, but they said, she seemed so deep in thought, she didn't hear them in time. What a waste, two lives taken. It looks like the elderly man in the car had a stroke. When he tried to push the brakes, he hit the gas pedal instead."

"I wonder if she has any family," the EMT driver said to Sergeant Fuller.

"We'll try to find out from her ID. I'm sure this will make the evening news. When we give her name, perhaps someone will contact us."

Sara's lawyer heard the news on TV and mailed the letter the next day.

Chapter 25 - Ethan's Observation

Nathan and Ethan were getting along well. The school had noticed some improvement in Ethan's behavior. His grades were still not good, but they were getting better.

Ethan hated to admit it but he had started looking forward to Wednesdays. Nathan had become a good friend. He had never met anyone like him. He was even getting used to church. He had surprised Mom and Emily last Sunday and gotten ready for church early and met them in the kitchen ready to go. Talk about a heart attack, he thought Mom was going to have one right there in the kitchen.

Nathan helped him come to grips with a lot of hang-ups. He had been so embarrassed about the things his dad had done that he had forgotten what was really important. He was angry and that anger was destroying his life as much as his dad had destroyed his own life. The sins might be different but they were producing the same results. There were so many things he was angry about: he no longer had a dad, Mom didn't have a husband, Mom had to work two jobs to support them, they had to leave their church shamed and he had to leave the school he had attended since kindergarten.

Making new friends was hard for him as he thought everyone knew about Dad and would not want to be his friend, so he had just become a jerk to keep from being rejected. He was very lonely and mad, mostly. That is, until he started hanging with Nathan.

Ethan could tell that Nathan was crazy about Charlotte. When they saw each other at church or when she joined them on their outing (she only came if it was something that would be fun for a girl), he could tell they loved each other. Charlotte seemed to be a very nice person and Ethan was sorry about what had happened to her. Watching her gave him hope. If she could get through that ordeal and come out happy and successful, perhaps there was hope for him.

Chapter 26 - Dying Grace

Charlotte could not remember ever being happier. Sure, she missed her dad but he was in a better place – all the suffering and anxiety gone forever. Mom was well and happy, working in the church. The Pastor had asked her to come by a couple days per week and work in the office. Since she worked part time at the tax office, it worked out well for her. She wouldn't be surprised if it became full time. Stephen and Debbie were doing wonderfully in Savannah. He loved teaching there and was finishing his second year. She had seen Thomas a few weeks ago and he was getting cuter and cuter, almost two now. And, then, of course, there was Nathan.

It was funny last week when one of her staff asked her about Nathan. She wanted her to talk about him so they could know the kind of man he is. Words; what are words? How do you describe perfection, she thought? Oh, she knew he wasn't perfect; but so far, she had not seen the imperfection. *What was it about him? His quiet strength - his loving compassion for others - his selflessness - his love for God - his humility - his blonde hair - his dimples - oh, I digress.* She had been daydreaming again and almost missed the phone ringing.

"Charlotte White speaking, how may I help you?"

"Come home, Charlotte, come home."

"Mom, what's wrong? Mom, Mom, are you there?"

Charlotte raced home wondering what had happened. She didn't know if she should call an ambulance or wait until she got to Mom. It wasn't like her to lose all control. Mom had always been the strong one in the family – the one with the most faith. A thousand scenarios ran through her mind.

Ella was in the rocker in the living room. She was sitting erect with her hands crossed over her heart. Tears were streaming down her face and her eyes were closed. "Mom, Mom," Charlotte sat on the ottoman and took her mother's hand in hers.

Ella opened her eyes and said, "Oh, Charlotte, they're gone, gone. Nothing could be done. It happened in an instant. They're gone."

"Who, Mom? Whose gone?"

"They said they were sorry to call and tell me. It was an automobile accident – head on with a big truck. They said they didn't suffer."

"Who, Mom? Who are you talking about?" Charlotte was afraid to hear the words but she needed to know. She called 911 for her mom and fixed her a cup of hot tea. She went back to her seat and took her mom's hands in hers and made her mom look her in the eyes. "Mom, I need you to tell me who called you."

"The hospital called…..the hospital in Savannah. I don't know which one."

"Okay, Mom, the hospital called. What did they say? Who did you talk to?"

"A doctor, yes, that's right, it was the doctor……. Stephen, Debbie, gone, gone."

Charlotte nearly passed out when she heard those words. She must keep her senses – she had to help Mom right now. She was in shock. Where is that ambulance?

Riding in the ambulance with her Mom, Charlotte dialed Nathan's number. She told him all she knew. He told her he would get on the phone and call all the hospitals in Savannah and find out what he could for her. He assured her he would meet her at the hospital with her mom.

The doctors had given her mom something for her nerves and she was sleeping, Charlotte sitting by her bed. They asked Charlotte if she needed something, but she refused. She wanted to be clear-headed when Nathan got there. *What was taking him so long, anyway?*

When she saw his face, she knew. "Oh, dear God, no, it's true, isn't it?"

"Charlotte, I'm so sorry. I got here as fast as I could. My motorcycle felt like it was flying in the air. The traffic was just horrendous....."

"Nathan, stop. Tell me what happened, tell me right now."

"Sit down, Charlotte. Let me get you some coffee or a pop," he said as he sat in the rocker in the room. "Yes, Stephen and Debbie were in a terrible, head-on collision with a semi-truck right at lunch time. I called the police in Savannah and they said they were killed instantly on impact. At least, we can be thankful for that."

"What about Thomas? Did they find him? Is he all right – maybe in his car seat in the back seat – maybe – maybe he," she couldn't finish.. "Not Thomas, too."

"Thomas is alive. He wasn't in the car. He was with a sitter at home. I talked with her on the phone. The police gave me Stephen's home number when I told him there was a child involved. The sitter said they were going to look for a second car for them as Debbie felt worried not having a car at home when he was at school. I guess they were on the expressway and the semi came across the median and hit them. She said she will keep Thomas at her home until we can get there. She gave me her address and phone number."

"Oh thank God.....thank God.....he's alive..... he's OK!"

Chapter 27 - Ethan finds peace

"Ethan, this is Nathan. Something happened and I won't be able to pick you up today. Charlotte's brother and sister-in-law have been killed and we have to head to Savannah right now. We're taking Ella and leaving as soon as the hospital discharges her. I will call you in a few days. Please pray for Charlotte and Ella. I know they would appreciate it."

"Tell her I'm sorry and I will pray for them. Please call me soon, Nathan."

Ethan set the phone back in the cradle in the school office and turned to leave. The secretary saw his countenance and knew something was wrong. "Ethan, can I help you? Has something happened to your mom?"

"No, nothing happened to Mom. A friend's brother and sister-in-law were just killed in a car accident in Savannah. That was my Big Brother calling to say he couldn't pick me up today for our outing. I can't believe I told him I would pray for them. I haven't prayed since I was a little boy. I don't know how. Why did I say I would? I don't think God would listen to my prayer anyway. You know my history here, I'm sure."

"Ethan, I am a Christian and I'll be glad to help you pray for them. Why don't you come into my office?"

How was it possible to feel so free, so alive, so forgiven? Ethan was so elated he had to tell someone. He knew his mom and sister would want to know. He couldn't wait to tell them. He had never thought it could be so simple, so complete. Miss Rogers, the secretary, had always been nice to him no matter how many times he had been sent to the principal. Now, he understood why. She was a Christian that really lived what she believed. She knew there was hope for him, she had said to him after he accepted Christ. She had faith in God and had prayed for him often. He did not realize so many people had been praying for him. He thought of Nathan and Charlotte and what they were going through right now. He stopped on his bike and bowed his head and prayed for them that God would be near and dear to them during this tragedy.

Ethan rode on rejoicing, when all of a sudden, he stopped and cried out, "Oh God, you want me to forgive my Dad, don't you?" He started weeping and sat down on the curb. How could he forgive his dad? After all he had done to their family, to Mom, to Emily – to him. No, he couldn't – not right now – he would need time – if he ever could do it.

Chapter 28 - Charlottes' confession

Thomas was asleep, finally. The past few days were just a blur to Charlotte and Nathan. Charlotte's mom had been sedated so heavily she was in bed most of the time. The sitter arrived and was ready to stay with Thomas while they attended the funeral.

"I can't get this hooked. Nathan, can you come help me? I seem to be all thumbs," Charlotte gently spoke as she prepared to leave for the church. "You do agree it is better not to take Thomas, don't you, Nathan?"

"I do agree with you, dear. He is not even two yet. He would not know anything happening and would probably get fretful and have to be cared for anyway.

This is going to be hard enough on you and Miss Ella as it is."

"Thank you, again, Nathan for staying here this week with us. I don't think I could have done it without you."

"There's no other place I could be this week than right here with you. I know how much Stephen and Debbie meant to you. No one could ever replace them but I want you and Ella to know I am here for you. Ella is grieving deeply. It's like she is in denial and cannot face the truth. I guess it will take some time and a lot of love from us to help her back on her feet."

Charlotte looked at this man so full of concern for her mom. "You know that you are a God-send to our family, don't you? I can't believe how you have taken care of Thomas – bathing, feeding, and playing with him. Do you know how much I love you?"

Nathan looked up from tying his shoe. Did Charlotte realize what she had just said to him? Perhaps it is from exhaustion and she isn't thinking clearly. He had loved her for months but had promised her long ago that if God wanted him to be just her friend and be a blessing to her in her new walk with Christ, he was willing to be that. Could she mean it – he could only hope. As he stood to his feet, he was wondering if now was the time to ask her about it.

Charlotte saw Nathan standing and staring at her. She wondered what was going through his mind. She knew she had shocked him. They had never spoken of love even though she had loved him for a long time. Throughout this week and the awful tragedy that had taken Stephen and Debbie, she became more and more convinced of her love for this man. She couldn't imagine a future without him. "It seems I shocked you, Nathan. Surely you know what you mean to me and my family."

"Of course, I know you and your mom love me. I just thought for a second that you meant something else. Sorry, I guess I had my hopes up."

"Really, Nathan, what did you think I meant?" It had been so long since they had laughed or teased each other. She was going to carry it a bit farther. They both needed to lighten up for the day that was ahead.

Nathan took a step toward this beautiful woman that he adored. He placed his hand on her cheek and gently lifted her chin toward him. "Oh, I don't know, Charlotte. I guess I was hoping against hope that you feel about me the way I feel about you," he said sincerely.

Charlotte realized this was not a time to play. "Yes, yes, yes, I do. I love you so much I feel my heart is going to jump right out of my body. I have wanted to tell you for so long but I knew we had that friendship thing going and I wasn't sure how you felt. I knew you were the best friend I ever had and I didn't want to take a chance on losing that if you didn't love me like I do you," Charlotte said as she laid her hand on his.

"Will you marry me, Charlotte White?" Nathan knew he had blurted it out without any style but he didn't care.

"Yes, Nathan, I will marry you. I was beginning to think I was going to be an old maid. I want to be your wife, your best friend, your help meet. You need to realize what you are getting into though. You know Thomas Stephen is my responsibility and Mom is not doing well at all. I don't know how long it will be before she smiles again. This is not going to be easy. Are you very sure this is what you want for the rest of your life?"

Nathan wrapped his long arms around her and lifted her from the floor turning her round and round. "You have made me the happiest man in this entire world. Yes, I want you and I want Thomas and I will help you with your mother the rest of her life. I give you my promise."

"Well, if I didn't know better, I'd believe there are two happy people in this room," Ella said standing at the door.

"Mom, Nathan just asked me to marry him and I said yes. Isn't that wonderful, Mom? Isn't he wonderful and handsome and awesome, Mom?"

Ella walked into the room and took each of them by the hand and placed them in her own hands. With tears in her eyes and a smile on her face she said, "This is something I have been praying for. I knew in my heart that you two were meant for each other but you kept on being friends so I never said anything. God is so good. In this tragedy, I lost my only son but today, He has given me another son to love and cherish. Can we pray right now before we have to go to the church and bury my precious boy and my sweet daughter in law?"

Nathan held the hands of the two women he loved the most in the world. He prayed that God would give them strength for the day and hope for tomorrow. He prayed for Thomas and for him and Charlotte that they would be great parents to him as he grew up and developed into a fine young man. He thanked God for Charlotte's love and thanked Him that she said yes to his marriage proposal and then they closed by saying the Lord's Prayer together.

Chapter 29 – The Announcement

It felt like the whole church was in their home today. Charlotte looked at Ethan who had shared his new found faith with them. Nathan hugged him and wept for joy. Emily was there with her mom, Paula. Chris and Jill were there to see Nathan. They were all excited about the new session starting in Operation Go at their church. They were telling Pastor Bob about it and getting him excited about starting it in his church. Charlotte hoped he would so she could have the opportunity to participate. That was one program that had changed the lives of those she loved standing around her. Charlotte looked over at Mom sitting on the couch holding Thomas. He was wrestling with her trying to get on the floor and go play. He was loved by everyone in attendance and had no trouble getting attention.

"We are happy to have each of you here today. Thank you for all the food and baked goods. We will be eating them for a month. We appreciate all your love and prayers for us during this difficult time. God has been so good to us through it all. Right now, I believe Nathan has something to tell you," Charlotte said as she stepped down from the stair and Nathan took her place on it. He grabbed her hand as she descended and spoke to the group.

"I am excited to tell you that I asked Charlotte to be my wife and she said yes. We are talking about a date and I think we have decided on a Christmas wedding. There is no greater gift I could receive that day than to become her husband and the father of precious Thomas. You are all invited to come. After all that has happened in recent days, we want a quiet ceremony at the church, Christmas day at 5:00 PM. We hope each of you will be there to share the joy of the day with us."

Chapter 30 – Paula' Decision

Ethan's life was so transformed that the Big Brother program was not needed for him anymore. He was telling the classmates at school what had happened to him and they could all see the difference in his life and his grades. His attitude was a 360 degree turn around. He was in church and youth activities and his mom was thrilled to see the change. Paula had come to the conclusion that it was time for her to take Ethan to see his dad. She didn't know how receptive he was going to be but she had to give it a try.

"Ethan, this Saturday, I'm driving into Atlanta to see your dad. I'd like it very much if you came with me."

"Mom, a few months ago, I would have said, 'No Way', but now – I think I can do it. If you can go, I can go," Ethan said quietly.

Chad was growing by leaps and bounds in the Word. Several Bible studies had been started and they were learning so much. Many of the prisoners came to know Christ and were witnessing to their visiting family members. It was like a revival had broken out in the Prison. Chad had stayed in contact with Chris and Chris shared with him the news of Charlotte's family and about her upcoming marriage to Nathan. He also told him that Ethan had become a Christian. Chad was so filled with joy that his son had come to Christ. He adored the Savior and all he wanted to do was tell others what Christ had done for him. Chad was writing about his life in a journal now and trying to understand the depth of the sin in which he had engaged. He was trying to figure out the beginning and had finally forgiven his own mom (something he thought he would never be able to do). He had, also, written letters to as many of the victims that he could find, asking for their forgiveness. Several had written back and said they had forgiven him while others wrote how their lives were ruined and it was his fault and they would never forgive him. He wrote to his church and apologized for the example he had been and asked them to pray for him as he served his much deserved punishment. The Pastor had been by a few times and prayed with him.

"Paula, you look wonderful. Ethan, please come and let me hug you. I am so happy for you. Chris told me you accepted Christ. I am so thankful to Chris and

Nathan and the church that came here to see us. So much has happened since that time that it makes my head spin when I think of all that have been saved since that first visit."

"Many wonderful things have happened, Chad. I wanted to come to tell you I have forgiven you, also. It has not been easy and it took me awhile, but I now see God cannot use me to His fullest purpose if I harbor hatred and bitterness toward anyone. Ethan's life is transformed and he truly is a new creature in Christ that the Bible talks about in II Corinthians 5:17."

"Thank you, Paula, for bringing Ethan to see me and thank you for coming, also. I don't deserve your forgiveness but I accept it. I did not deserve God's forgiveness and He forgave me and washed me clean. There's so much I need to say to you, Paula. Do you mind if I write you some letters and just talk about what happened and what is happening now in my life?"

"I think that would be a wonderful thing, Chad. I can see how you have changed just from spending this little time together. I would like to get to know the real Chad now. I would be happy to read and answer your letters. Ethan, did you have something you wanted to say to your dad?"

"Dad, I was so happy you were my dad when I was little. It was years before I knew of any of the problems you had. Mom never talked bad about you, even after they took you to jail. I hated you so much and I couldn't understand how she could still defend you to us. Even after I was saved, I told God I could not forgive you.

It has been several months now and Nathan has been through a lot of the Bible with me. He helped me see that I can never be my best for God until I have settled this matter with you. Dad, it still hurts me when I think of all the wasted years that we could have had as a family and how I still have to go to school and play sports and never have my dad there to watch me play and Dad, it does hurt. But Dad, I came to say I have forgiven you. I know it will take me some time to forget the pain and start loving you again, but I have forgiven to the best of my ability at this point. Can you live with that for now, Dad?"

Chad grabbed his son and held him close. He took Paula's hand in his and the three of them prayed to the heavenly Father, together.

Chapter 31 – Charlotte faces her giant

She was so nervous. Just two weeks and she was going to be Nathan's wife. It was so exciting but scary also. She wished she had not said yes when Nathan told her where they were going today. More than anything in life, she did not want to face Chad Everett today. Yes, she knew she had to – it was the right thing to do. She did not want to start out a new life with part of the old one hanging on.

When she saw him standing in the visiting room with his hands in his pockets and his head bowed low, she had the strangest sensation that she had never met this man. He looked so different than she remembered or perhaps finally her memory of him was fading. She knew in her heart she would be able to do this.

"I will be right beside you all the way," Nathan assured her as the doors to the visiting area opened.

"Thanks Nathan, but suddenly there is a quiet calmness in me that I can't explain. It must be the power of the Holy Spirit at work in my life and in Chad's. I'm glad that you are with me. I have a feeling everything is going to be all right," Charlotte told him as they stepped through the door.

"Charlotte, thank you for coming here today. There are no words to express my appreciation. Let me say, first thing, how sorry I am for what I put you through in your life. The pain and humiliation I caused you is unforgivable. I won't blame you if you never forgive me, but my prayer is that someday you can find it in your heart to do so."

"Chad, if someone had told me a year ago that I would be standing in the same room with you speaking civilly to you, I would have laughed in their face. God has also been working mightily in my life. You would not believe the things that have happened to help me turn to Him with my whole heart. I never realized this kind of relationship was available with anyone. He is my dearest friend and confidant. He has given me a wonderful man that loves me and loves God. We have a precious little boy that we will have the joy of rearing together as our son. Truly, His ways are not our ways. It is true, I would not have chosen the path that has been given me, but I know now that He knows what is best for me. All the pain, loneliness and heartache I experienced has taught me so many principles that God is using in my life now to be a blessing to others. I don't think I would have ever been able to do the things He has allowed me to accomplish had I not endured that pain and suffering."

Chad was weeping openly now and sat down in the chair with his head bowed. Charlotte thought he was praying so she and Nathan sat down quietly and didn't speak. In a moment or two, he lifted his head and looked calmly at them. "This will be the best Christmas I will have ever had. My life has always been a sham, a life of pretending. I am so undeserving of your forgiveness. I guess you heard that Paula and Ethan came to see me and we are making our way back together as a family. I know it will be a long time before I am out of this place, but; I know that God has a plan for me and I am going to stay with His plan until He has another one for me. Thank you so much for seeing me today and I wish you all the happiness you deserve. I will pray for you and Nathan and the little one as you raise him for God. My regret for the rest of my life will be the memory of the awful sins I committed against you, against God, my wife and my children. I know I am forgiven and it is under the blood, but it will always be a part of my memory that I have to live with and seek His victory for my life."

They said their goodbyes and when they left that building and stepped out in the cool fresh air, Charlotte felt young and innocent again. It was something she could not explain so she kept it to herself, for now. She was very excited about getting married and starting her life with Nathan and Thomas. She looked at Nathan and sensed that he knew what she was thinking. He always seemed to know what she was thinking and she was glad. Charlotte smiled and stepped into the car, leaned her head back. Suddenly she felt like singing Christmas carols, "Deck the halls with boughs of holly, fa la la la la la la la la." She looked over at Nathan and he was grinning from ear to ear!

Chapter 32 - TEN YEARS LATER

"Pastor Nathan, thank you for inviting me to your anniversary party. It is only fitting we hold it here at this church," Ethan said to Nathan.

"We are just glad you could get away from school this weekend. I hear you are nearly finished your Doctorate in theology. Do you know yet where God wants you to serve?"

"No, not exactly, but since this church has grown so much in the last five years since you have been the pastor, I would love to come here and help you with the evangelistic outreach program and teach a Sunday School class for teenagers. Do you think you might have any interest in my working for you?"

"Charlotte and I would be very excited about that. You know Thomas is twelve now and God is working in that little heart of his. I believe you could be a strong, positive influence on him. I know your mom would be happy to have you back again. I understand your dad had a parole hearing recently and it looks favorable for him to be released in the next few months. I guess you are happy about that, also."

"What are you two up to now?" Charlotte reached up to straighten the collar of her husband's shirt and smiled into his loving face, "Your princess, Joanna, says she is ready for some ice cream."

"I don't think I have ever met a cuter four-year-old in my life," Ethan said to Joanna. She, of course, giggled with delight at her new found friend. Nathan left to find the ice cream for he and Joanna.

"Your husband just asked me how I felt about Dad getting paroled. I want to ask you that same question," Ethan said to Charlotte.

"You know, Ethan, my life is so complete now, I don't think there is anything that could change that for me. We are happy working in the church together, seeing folks coming to Christ on a regular basis, the joy of having our precious daughter, my Mom still in pretty good health over at the assisted living center which Emily is now in charge of, and doing a great job, I hear. No, I will not have any problem if he is released and I know it will make your mom happy. She has waited so faithfully for him. She deserves some years of happiness. I have no bitterness toward Chad. Your mom has shared some of the things that happened to him as a child and that puts a different perspective on it for me."

"Thank you, Charlotte for saying those kind words. As I have grown in the Lord in the last ten years, I find I have completely forgiven Dad and look forward to spending time with him. I'm sorry my wife, Faye, could not be here today. You know she has just given birth to Austin last week and we were afraid the trip would be too much for her."

Charlotte sat on the porch late in the day, all the guest were gone. Nathan had left to take Thomas and Joanna to see their grandmother. She would go by tomorrow. She was happy to be here alone with her thoughts. She was so thankful she had never told Chad or his family about the baby she gave away. The adoptive family had sent her pictures over the years. They had written a few years ago that Elizabeth (that was her name) wanted to know her birth mother. She had encouraged them not to tell her yet with everything that was going on at the time. Perhaps now that Elizabeth was grown with her own life now, it might be a good time to meet her. She knew Nathan would be good with it and that Joanna and Thomas would like having a sister. She wanted to pray more on it since it would affect Paula, Emily, Ethan and Chad. Life had gone full circle now – she remembered the day Ethan had been born and how her life changed forever that day. Now, he and his wife had a precious son, Austin, God had blessed them with. Through all the pain and heartache, she was thankful God never left her alone, but sent her a special friend when she needed him most. Then to top it all off, turned that friend into her loving husband, the father of her children and her pastor. God is so good!